Behind Enemy Lines

JEANNE ADAMS

This is a work of fiction. Names, characters, organizations, places, events, and incidents are either products of the author's imagination or are used fictitiously.

Published by Jeanne Adams

ISBN-0989444066
ISBN-13: 978-0-989-4440-6-4

DEDICATION

This book is dedicated to "The Greatest Generation" – the men and women who served in the Second Great War - to protect global freedom.
They set a standard which we still strive to match.

A Special salute to
James H. Pickering,
US Army Medical Corps, European Theatre
O. William Adams,
US Navy, Pacific Theatre
Ralph G. Dowling,
US Army ,Pacific Theatre
Hadley B. Phillips,
Merchant Marine, Pacific Theatre
Victor W. Adams, Jr,
US Army, Pacific Theatre
James A McDowell
US Army, European Theatre

.

CONTENTS

ACKNOWLEDGMENTS

To my Sultry Sisters, Barbara Devlin and Caitlenn T Ainnsley, THANK YOU! It was so fun to imagine this series with you, to work it out and get it out, each in our respective time periods.
Thank you, too, to PE for the formatting and uploading assistance. You, as always, ROCK!
To Lyndsey Lewellen, the cover design is beyond fabulous..

CHAPTER ONE

15th November 1939
The Lady Grace Corvedale
Charelton Wineries
5, rue de Pretres Saint-Germaine
Paris
Dearest Sister,

I trust all is well at the Paris office. Enclosed is a note from Lord Bittebrug regarding the rare Calvados brandy he requires. He's authorized purchase and travel, as he demands it straight away. I know it's earlier than expected, but if you bring the full account books, we'll go over them now, saving you bringing them at the holiday. In that fashion, we shall fully enjoy the festivities instead of being harnessed to dusty tomes of figures!

Best,
Char
Viscount Charelton
Charelton Wineries

Grace read the note from her brother with a

deepening frown. As far as she knew, the only Lord Bittebrug they'd ever encountered was a horse who'd bitten Char when they were children. Char had complained about the brute for weeks, nursing both bruise and grudge with equal ferocity.

Hoping for enlightenment, she unfolded the second page of heavy, cream-colored card stock, which featured a lettermark at the top from one of London's finest clubs.

Dear Lady Corvedale,

I was most pleased to receive word from your brother that you had obtained the location of the rare 1902 Coeur de Tigre brandy I requested. Per Lord Charleton's note to me with price and transportation costs, I send this missive to authorize its purchase.

While I know you may have a regular route to London from Pays-Auge, due to the price I am paying for this rare brandy, I ask that you take Lord Southerly's coach train rather than a motor car. Your brother assures me you've taken this route before, whilst still in boarding school. I fear the unholy jostling from a motor might damage the brandy, for which I'm paying so dearly.

I look forward to seeing you, and the product, in the next few days.

With sincere appreciation,
The Honorable Phineas Bittebrug

Grace let herself slide into her chair. This, then, was the warning she'd been expecting. This charade of a letter, written in clandestine fashion to avoid German interception, told her to get out of France now, while she still could.

The rumbles of another great war had rolled like

thunder over Europe for the last three years. England, France and Germany were now officially at war. Poland had been attacked, and taken.

Now the storm of that brewing conflict was upon her. She, like her late Uncle Phineas during the first Great War, must quit France in haste.

Grace clutched the pendant, which lay out of sight under her blouse. While its gems and rich old gold were covered by the conservative starched India cotton blouse and silk jacket she wore for work, its reassuring weight gave her courage. She usually wore it openly as a brooch on her lapel or on lace at her throat, but for some reason today, she'd slid the chain through the loop on the back and hidden it.

Still holding it, she made her mental list. She must pack her clothes, and the diary—nearly as precious as the gems around her neck—as well as the account books for the winery. From there, she would head north. Char had given her the perfect out on that one. She already had a ticket for next month's train and ferry for her Christmas visit.

She'd planned to make that her quarterly accounting with Char to go over the books, and her staff in Paris knew it. She had money at her flat, of course. Once in Calais, she had contacts if she needed them.

Contacts Char knew nothing about.

Between the standard route and making a flat out run for it, she would still be covered.

"Lord Southerly's Coaching route," she said aloud, laughing in spite of the dire news. "Yes, that's just the thing."

She'd used that very method to escape her stuffy French boarding school twice. After the second time she'd masqueraded as Lady Southerly, a widow in mourning, and had gotten all the way to Calais, her father, Lord Standish, had relented and let her come home to London to finish her education.

The antique train coaches on "Lord Southerly's Line" catered to the gentry and offered the utmost in old-fashioned luxury. It was discreet transportation, which ran at odd, and somewhat unpredictable intervals, following the whims of its wealthy patrons.

The laughter faded as quickly as it had come. She had a lot of work to do.

France had declared war, lest they violate their treaties with Poland, but was, nominally, still neutral. That neutrality faded with each passing day. Troops were already massing in the north, bracing for the onslaught they knew would come.

Rumors of a German annexation, or outright invasion, swirled constantly. Suspicion of collusion was ripe within every business deal, every contract. Even the wineries with which she dealt weren't immune.

Spies were everywhere, and as a British citizen, it was going to take every skill she had to get out.

If she was followed, or they attempted to detain her...

Grace grimaced at the aura of superior, smug condescension that had greeted her at one estate where she'd been just a week ago. There had been a group of German buyers there, tasting this year's vintages.

She had other business there, clandestine business, thanks to her father. With that and the German presence, it had taken her a week to relax afterward.

She reopened the letter she'd completed prior to

receiving the missive from her brother. She peeled off the old-fashioned wax seal and snapped it before she dropped it in the dust bin. Below the standard listing she'd compiled of purchases and thoughts on the wine harvest, she added a post script.

Dearest Char,

Received your post and the scrawl from Lord Phineas. I owe you a shilling as I've lost my bet with you that the old goat wouldn't cough up the money for that bottle.

I'll head out for Pays-Auge and the seller's estate in two days, then get the coach. I'd rather take the regular train but Lord B would probably check my ticket and demand a discount.

Best,

Grace

There, that would tell him that she'd gotten the message, and the bit about the bet would tell him where to pick her up. They'd only bet a shilling one time. They'd been teenagers, and Char bet her she wouldn't walk into a dockside bar in Portsmouth.

Neither of them had thought about the danger, they'd simply done it, then laughed and laughed when their father, horrified, had come to drag them out of the bar for the ferry ride to Calais. Char had gotten the strap for that one, and she'd been given an endless lecture about the damnable hazard of gambling.

"Gambling is a sin of the utmost danger to your soul, to your family," she mocked her father's pompous tones. The words rang out in the echoing silence of her office. "For always, it leads you to believe you are not at risk."

Grace's grandfather, her father's father, had nearly

bankrupted the family through gambling, so His Lordship had reason to despise it.

She lit a match and resealed the letter with a fresh wax wafer and her seal. She would post it on her way to her suite of rooms.

She'd just put the seal away when her secretary knocked briefly, then bustled in with a sheaf of papers. Her abrupt entry made Grace jump, but she forced herself to relax. She had to act as if it were business as usual, as if she were going to make a little trip north, purchase a brandy, then jaunt over the channel to deliver it. Something she did with surprising regularity.

She'd lie and say she'd be back at her desk in Paris in a few days. It wasn't as if she hadn't become used to the deceptions. This time, however, there was an underlying ache.

She was deeply saddened to leave. Despite her horrible experience in boarding school, she loved France. She loved the people, the food, the wonderful nightlife, and of course, the wine.

"Eh, Elisette," she said to the secretary in flawless, schoolbook French. "I must go to Pays-Auge, then home for a few days to deliver that 1902 brandy we found for the client. I'm taking the account books now so I can do my quarterly reporting early. I'll be back by," Grace paused to consult her gilt-edged calendar. "Monday at the latest. If my father doesn't insist I dance attendance on him at Dale Manor, I'll stay the weekend and see some of my chums in London, then head back. If he does, then it may be Wednesday before I'm back, but no later than that."

"*Oui*, Lady Corvedale," Elisette made a note, and looked up expectantly. "Do you need me to make your travel?"

"No, my brother took care of it and charged it to the buyer," she made herself grin at Elisette, inviting her to share the joke of pawning the expense off on the client. Elisette dutifully laughed, but Grace caught the calculation in her eyes.

The last shred of doubt disappeared. Elisette was reporting her movements to someone. That look sealed it.

Damn it all.

The secretary left to carry out the morning's business, but Grace waited a heartbeat to be sure she wasn't coming back in. The ornate ormolu clock chimed the hour from its place of honor on a nearby bombe chest.

Carefully and quietly, Grace rose and crossed the room. She turned the key in the door's lock and settled in for some serious work.

There was a lot to do before she left the office, much less the country.

Lt. Robert "Dix" Dixon shrugged out of his overcoat and acted as if he handed such mundane things off to a stiff, uniformed English butler every day. In America, few families kept this kind of "high" servant, even if they were wealthy. At least they didn't in New Orleans. There were butlers there, sure, but not this kind.

Dix took off his cover, and handed the stiff officer's cap to the man as well.

"Thank you," he said, and the butler nodded, but said nothing in reply. He then followed his friend Char into the depths of the opulent townhouse. The weight of centuries hung around the building's graceful architecture, but the furnishings were of the latest mode. That is, until he arrived in the Marquis' office.

"It's been five days since she should have been at Portsmouth," Arthur Corvedale, Lord Charleton--Char to his friends--stated the obvious as he paced his father's study. Dix's friend had hardly introduced Dix before he leapt on the obvious. "Something's happened, Father. Grace is never late. Ever."

"I'm aware of that," Char's father, Lord Michael Standish, Marquis of Dale, intoned, glancing at the fourth man in the room. Lord Shippingston nodded, but Dix had no idea what he was approving.

"There is little, officially, that we can do," Standish continued.

When Char protested, his father held up a meaty hand. "Officially. We are newly at war, Arthur." Obviously Char's father didn't use the nickname. "Things are unsettled, unpredictable. Officially, we begin a search for her and hire an investigator in France, and so forth." He waved the same hand, dismissing all that *regular* nonsense. "We'll do more than that, of course."

Relief eased over Char's features. But from Standish's body language, Dix guessed this was far more serious than one overdue girl.

As proof of his hunch, the Marquis continued. "We are all aware that this is not a regular disappearance."

Char froze in the act of lighting a cheroot and a cold ball of dread settled into Dix's gut. That feeling always told him he was heading into serious danger.

Char had invited Dix to accompany him to Portsmouth when he picked up Grace. Dix had wanted to see the port anyway, so he'd gone.

The more he knew, the better he could plan. In his capacity as an unofficial American attaché to the British War Office in London, he was, officially, a nonentity. A cipher.

His real, clandestine duties were a whole lot more interesting.

They'd waited two days in Portsmouth. When the sister didn't arrive, Char had driven at breakneck speed back to London to call on his father, the Marquis.

Char had intimated his father was involved in *Special Projects* with the Home Office. Dix had met the Marquis briefly at the Home Office, but now was not the time to reveal that.

"I am well aware of Grace's movements," the Marquis said, looking drained. "She did not reach The Suffolk Special. I had hoped some of her other resources would have allowed her to get to Portsmouth, however."

"Oh, Father, what have you done?" Char spun to confront his father. "How could you? How could you involve Grace in your doings?"

Lord Shippingston cleared his throat, and Char blushed. Dix fully expected Char's father to take Char to task for speaking so bluntly in front of Lord Shippingston.

Instead, the Marquis looked at Shippingston, and again, Shippingston nodded.

Char's imposing father sighed heavily, suddenly looking every one of his nearly sixty years. The defeated slump of Standish's otherwise fiercely erect posture, however slight, pulled Dix's attention away from Shippingston and back to Char's father.

"What?" Char demanded, staring at his father.

"Grace volunteered, Char. Insisted, in fact," Standish said heavily. He continued as he ponderously rose to pour himself a brandy. "However, we can only seem to look for her through official channels. That hasn't changed. We'll proceed in the ways I've mentioned."

"Unofficially, then?" Char snapped, out of patience with his father's machinations.

Dix didn't know the girl, but he could hardly believe Standish would allow this Grace, who was Char's *younger* sister, to involve herself in Home Office plots and schemes...

"Grace is a law unto herself, Arthur," the older man said sharply. "We have ideas as to how to locate her. We'll be calling on your friend," Standish nodded toward Dix, and Char's frown turned stormy and angry. "To help us."

"What does Dix have to do with this?"

"He's far more than an unofficial attaché, boy," Standish snapped. Shippingston *ahem-ed* again and now Standish turned his pique on the hefty diplomat. "Do you have something to add?"

Shippingston looked briefly surprised, then simply smiled.

"Not at all. I was merely thinking you might want to let both our guests change, and adjourn this until after dinner."

As he spoke, the clock chimed the hour and Standish looked surprised. "Ah, it's grown late. Yes, you are correct."

"But father--" Char began.

"No, Lord Shippingston is correct. Lt. Dixon, I believe Lord Charleton will have evening wear to fit you." He eyed Dix's uniform for a moment. "Hmm. I'll tell Willoughby to send up the suit your cousin Henry left," he said to Char. Turning back to Dix, he ordered, more than asked. "You'll join us for dinner, I trust?"

"Of course, sir. I'd be honored."

"We'll send a note to your commanding officer to let him know you're in our care," Standish said with a weary smile. "As well as a note to our other colleagues," he added with a sharper look.

"Thank you, sir."

With a look of disbelief mixed with irritation, Char made a slight bow to his father and led Dix from the room.

They'd barely reached Char's room in the massive town house when Char burst out with, "What the hell was that about."

"I told you. Attaché is a ruse. I'm here for a lot of reasons that have nothing to do with paperwork and horse fairs." The last part was a bit of dig, since Char's duty to show him some of the RAF facilities had digressed into a jaunt to a championship horse show and sale.

"Spies and secrets," Char growled. "You and Standish might actually be worse than my sister."

"Your sister's a spy?"

Char snorted as he undid his collar. "Of course. And this isn't her first foray to get information for Father's little *projects*. I think she did her first work for the Crown when she was barely eighteen."

"How old is she now?"

"Oh, only twenty-three, and barely that," Char finally smiled. "But she was born to sneak and spy."

Char's man knocked on the door and came in with

a perfectly pressed evening suit, leaving it to hurry away and polish Dix's already highly polished shoes.

The suit provided was, thankfully, larger than anything Char might have had. Dix was much bigger through the chest and shoulders. Cousin John--whoever he might be--was obviously closer to Dix's breadth of chest. The formal kit, though a bit snug, sufficed.

They were heading down to dinner when Char again spoke of his sister. "You've got to understand, Dix. Grace is brilliant. I'm actually not surprised she demanded father cut her into the action, given her sneaky ways. She's a whiz with ciphers and codes, she is. But..."

"You're worried. It's understandable," Dix didn't know what else to say. A woman alone in what was, essentially, a war zone. If it had been *his* sister...

He laughed at the image. His sister would never survive as a clandestine agent. Sophia was too bold. Too...impulsive.

"If she's as sneaky as you say, then she'll come out all right," Dix said, trying to inject a positive note into the words. "Hopefully we'll get a cable from Portsmouth in the morning cursing us for making her wait."

Char smiled faintly, obviously unconvinced. "We can only hope."

They entered the dining room, only to find Standish and Shippingston with a uniformed stranger.

"She's waitin' on Hitler, in Germany," the man stammered.

CHAPTER TWO

"The hell you say!" Char burst out. Dix was thinking the same thing.

"Hush," Standish said. Turning back to the messenger he said, "Go on."

"She was taken sir, before she could get on the train. Evidently it was peaceful-like, if you take my meanin', but word is she's detained waitin' on the Führer. He wants a word with her fer some reason."

"Where is this?" Shippingston said sharply.

The messenger turned his way. "Zweiwig," he said, then stopped. "No, Zweiburg, he said. "It's over the border in'ta Germany a bit. At a hunting lodge."

"Dammit!" Standish paced angrily up a few paces, then back. "If she were still in France we could act openly." He turned to Dix. "I guess we'll still need you, young man."

Shippingston took the documents the messenger handed to him, dismissing him to go back to the Home Office. Shippingston tucked the papers into his breast pocket and moved to sit.

"We might as well eat, then plan. No use planning on an empty stomach."

Dix thought otherwise, but sat with the others as a multi-course meal was served. Again, he acted as if this level of formality was his norm. It wasn't.

Inwardly he smiled at the thought of his fiery, impatient, half-Cherokee father sitting through such nonsense. Beauregard Dixon entertained lavishly, and often, but he never let it get in the way of business.

But Dix was adept at blending in, and fitting in, without becoming totally invisible. And tonight, that meant having an elegant dinner and waiting for his mission orders.

Evidently this Lady Grace Corvedale was important enough to send someone--Dix—-in to fetch her. Given that, he needed all the information possible on Lady Grace Corvedale.

He'd already set up exit points for both American and British citizens when the time came for them to be evacuated from France. That was ready. After Poland's forced annexation, war was declared. Despite their building efforts, there was doubt France would hold the line against German forces. The United States was nominally neutral. For now. But agents from both countries would need ways to get out when the time came.

He just hoped he could get himself and this English socialite out of Germany before the hammer came down.

Grace paced the room at the old hunting lodge. Her possessions had been returned to her, all but the diary that went with her brooch. That, the German general had kept.

As polite as he was, Herr General Freisenstadt was not nice. The hard set of his mouth and the coldness in his eyes told her he wasn't a man to be trifled with.

To her great surprise, he hadn't taken the brooch. She was still wearing it as a pendant, concealed beneath her shirt.

There had been no other questions. Nothing about the other trips she'd made. There was no mention of the English presence in France. Nothing was asked about the many jaunts she'd made over the various borders, now war zones.

In fact, Herr General's questions had been brief. And all about her brooch.

Just the jewel. And the diary.

And of course, in his cold, but pleasant and courteous manner, he had answered none of her questions.

Irritated, she took another turn around the room trying to get past her immense anger and get to something constructive. She had to escape, of course.

The first day, she'd been driven here. Then she'd been fed, and kept locked in the room ever since. The servants had been obsequious, even welcoming, but adamant in their refusal to discuss her situation.

She conned enough German to know that she was being held until Adolf Hitler himself arrived to talk to her. Somehow he'd learned about her antique jeweled brooch, and the legend around it, and around her family's ancient Templar origins.

Grace's lip curled in a silent snarl. It wasn't like anyone had kept the legend secret, exactly. Each generation's eldest daughter, if there was one, received the brooch. The previous generation's eldest daughter passed it on to her daughter, or to the niece or cousin she felt should be the recipient. Grace's Aunt, also named Grace, had passed it to her namesake on the day Grace turned eighteen.

Aunt Grace's brood was large, but they were all boys.

Grace didn't really believe in the legend. How could dreaming of your "destined love" be helpful in any way? And really. Different dreams? Compelling futures?

Balderdash. But she loved the jewel, and kept the tradition of wearing it, always. And because she did that bit, she kept the journal with her at all times, as well.

Grace looked at her watch as she heard the creaking of the great stairs down the hall from her room. There was a perfunctory knock and the grate of a key in the old fashioned lock.

The same pattern had been repeated for three days now. She'd been here a week, but within the last few days, three more generals had arrived. She'd been introduced, but then sequestered in her room.

She'd smelled the luscious scent permeating the house, and heard the talk echoing up from the living areas below. Now, dinner was about to be served.

She hurried to the chair by the window and picked up the book she'd left there. She wanted always to appear unconcerned about her situation, confident that all was well, that her release was imminent.

She preserved the illusion that she was an honored guest.

"Fräulein Corvedale, your dinner."

A woman, the lodge's housekeeper, bustled in. Her name was Frau Shemper and she spoke superb

English. "Come, come, I will set it up here, yes?" She motioned the servant following her to put the tray down on the table near where Grace sat.

As he set down the tray, the man watched her. Harsh white scars ran like claw marks under a black eye patch. His stooped posture and distinct limp should have made him look menacing.

Instead, there was a knowing look in his good eye, an assessing look. It was as if he wanted--needed--to talk to her, but dared not.

"It won't be long now," Frau Shemper chirped chattily, pulling the curtains, shutting out the winter landscape. "The generals, they meet in the dining room tonight, so I've brought your dinner. But, tomorrow night our special guests will be here," the woman said, her smile twinkling, inviting Grace to enjoy the idea of that. "You will enjoy this, yes? Leaving the room, of course. And to come downstairs, wearing one of the lovely gowns I pressed for you. Yes, yes," Frau Shemper said, beaming, her hands clasped together. "It will be good."

Dinner tonight was a hearty stew with crusty bread laid in a lovely wooden bowl with a snowy linen cloth. The smell of it made Grace's stomach give an unladylike growl.

There was a bottle of wine, a red, to go with the stew, as well as a fat pot of tea, a cream pitcher and sugar bowl. The sight of those made her sigh.

She'd almost made it. She'd gotten to Calais. She'd almost made the ferry. They'd let her get as far as the first class waiting lounge before they pounced. The tea she'd ordered arrived with three Nazi officers. If she'd seen the barest whisker of them before she arrived at the ferry, she'd have melted into the crowd and disappeared without a trace.

Evidently they'd guessed that.

"*Danke*, Frau Shemper."

"*Bitte-bitte.* Of course, of course," Frau Shemper replied, as she turned to smooth the bed covers and plump the pillows. The manservant had tended the fire, and now stood at the door, a hulking, dark-haired reminder that she was a prisoner.

His presence sent a shiver down her back, which she disguised by rising from her seat, moving to the newly awakened fire. There was something about him...something compelling.

Under her shirt, the jeweled pendant shifted against her skin. It was a warm and reassuring weight. Somehow, she'd get out of here.

Grace had been well trained, and her self-defense skills were superb. Unfortunately, even if she could take out both Frau Shemper and the manservant, there was a guard in the hall, and another patrolling the lower floor. Yet another guard walked a beat in the garden, with one at the gate, and at least one at the end of the drive, which she could see from her windows.

"Come, now, Fräulein. You must be hungry, yes?"

Grace realized she'd been staring off into space. "Yes, of course. Thank you, Frau Shemper, for bringing dinner up yourself. You must be very busy with such important guests to tend."

"Ja, ja." Frau Shemper beamed at the implied compliment. "But you, too, are an important guest, Fräulein."

Knowing it was useless to remind the woman she was a prisoner, Grace sighed.

"*Danke.* The stew smells heavenly. I believe I'll

continue to enjoy my book as I eat, Frau Shemper."

Under Frau Shemper's approving eye, Grace took a seat at the little table, taking up the napkin to put in her lap.

"Good, good. I will send Franz back for the tray in three-quarters of an hour, yes?" The woman beamed more broadly as Grace picked up the spoon. "Enjoy, yes? Good. There is much for me to see to before our other guests arrive."

She bobbed a curtsey before she bustled out of the room. The manservant gave Grace one more penetrating look as he too backed out of the door with a bow. The lock turned once more and the only sound in the room was the crackle of the freshly stoked fire.

Grace hurried to the door, dropping down to peer under the gap. Frau Shemper's sturdy shoes were nowhere to be seen, but the manservant's well-worn boots and the guard's highly polished Hessians were visible. She strained to hear what the two men were saying.

Something about his boots tugged at her subconscious, but she pushed it aside as she strained to hear their conversation.

"...back for the tray?"

"Half'n hour or so," the deeper voice had a rough quality to it, as if the manservant had a rasp in his throat. His German must be a local dialect as it was guttural and hard to understand.

"Be sure to take all the silverware," the guard joked. "Don't want her attacking you, now do we?"

There was some kind of growling response from the manservant. The guard answered in kind, low and masculine, but she couldn't catch the words. What she did catch was the tone and the way both men laughed.

Grace sat back on her heels, frowning. That was the kind of laughter men shared when they were making ill remarks about a woman.

Damn. This was quite the pickle.

She returned to her stew. It was delicious, and she ate every scrap. She would have eaten it even if had it been horrid. Food meant strength. When she escaped, she might not safely find food until she was back across the border into France. Better to eat as heartily as she could now.

She stared out the window at the tall pines, simple cutout shapes outlined in contrast to the cold winter sky. There was a dusting of snow on the ground, and Grace could see mountains in the distance. The location of the lodge, miles over the German border, was a mystery. But she'd counted the time, and speed, from the border post to the lodge. She had figured twenty miles give or take a few miles.

If she could get out and away, she could manage twenty miles. It wouldn't be easy, but to escape this? Oh, yes. She could do it.

What could Hitler want with her? With the jewel? She didn't want to think about the diary. She prayed it was still in the lodge, that she could find it. Though not as ancient as the brooch, it told only the stories of the women in her family who'd possessed the jewel through the centuries.

It was a story book, but a precious one. Those stories, magical or not, were her history, her people. She couldn't be the one to break that chain and lose the book.

She smiled as she poured a cup of tea and

prepared it to her liking. The journal's stories were fanciful, full of love and longing and angst.

Even her aunt's entry...Grace hesitated over that memory. She knew her aunt and uncle's story. And the entry told all that, and so much more.

Still. They were stories. Fables.

If it were only that, well, it wouldn't be so dangerous. Unfortunately, she'd used it to create a code system. She stored her notes in it, and had given her father the key to the code and told her aunt that if anything happened to her, Standish must see the book before it was passed on to the next oldest Corvedale daughter.

"Lovely thoughts, Grace," she chided herself. She wasn't dead yet, and the lock on the bedroom door was ridiculously simple. She could pick it in less than a minute.

That thought had her setting the wine aside. Still, she couldn't resist reading the label

For other meals, she'd been served wines from Alsace-Lorraine, close to Moselle, which Germany and France had traded back and forth in successive wars through the centuries.

This, however, was a regional French vineyard she'd visited. One closer to the German border.

"That bastard," she said, slapping the bottle onto the table. It was clear, now, how Hitler had heard about the brooch. This vintner's wife had asked about it two or three seasons back. On her visit there this year, in July, the vintner himself brought up the legend of her jeweled brooch.

"Now I know. Dammit," she cursed softly. She was furious with herself. She'd told the story as a way to gain the confidence of the vintner's wife, to build rapport. She'd hoped to tap the woman for information. She had, over the last few years, gained the wife's trust. That trust was signified by an invitation to the youngest daughter's wedding to a neighboring vintner in the spring.

During the July visit, she'd garnered significant information about troop movements and the illegal billeting of German soldiers in homes not far from the vineyard. She knew the build-up heralded the invasion of France. The information was vital, so she couldn't regret what she'd said to get it, but...

She lost track of time, as she sat brooding by the fire. The heavy tread in the hallway and subsequent scrape of the key in the lock startled her. She rose, expecting Frau Shemper.

The manservant was alone. He left the door open and Grace assessed her chances.

"I wouldn't try it, Lady Corvedale," the man said, his voice low and controlled. He spoke English!

An American! Within seconds she recognized the tenor of the accent, if not the exact area of that vast, raw country.

"What did you say?" As she watched, he transformed, standing taller, looking leaner and less bulky as he stood straight. His shoulders, already broad, were even bigger when he stood up to his full height, his posture exact and erect.

"Don't try to jump me and I won't have to hurt you."

She sneered, bluffing. It could be a trap.

"As if I were considering it? What do you take me for, sir?"

"A smart, dangerous woman." He chuckled to soften the words, but kept it to a whisper of sound.

"I recognize someone sizing up a target. Let's just say Lord Bittebrug won't get his brandy, shall we?"

"Why would an American care?" she hissed, and had the satisfaction of seeing his eyes narrow.

She moved to the table, putting the empty tea things back onto the tray. That let her edge over and keep him on her left. That put the table between them, gave her weapons.

His words were a good opening gambit, but she was suspicious. Her letter had been intercepted, without a doubt. How else would the Nazis have caught her?

"Ah," he replied, taking a step closer, watching her with the one, dark, fierce eye. "An American would care if he knew your brother, and had gone with Char to Portsmouth to win a shilling."

"Many people know him. He's quite social, inviting near strangers to come along and see horses, or cars, or views." She dismissed that. That too could have been extrapolated from the letter.

The chuckle returned. "Yes, he is all that. Remind me to tell you about the horse he conned me into buying. I'm going to name it Shippingston."

Surprise hit her, and she reached up to grip the jewel in an unconscious gesture. The feel of it reassured her, its heat warmed her hand.

How close to the fire had she been sitting for it to be so warm?

Watching her warily, the man picked up the teapot and poured cold tea on the floor.

"Why did you do that?"

"Hush," the man hissed, cocking his head. When no sound came from the hall, he continued. "Char told me you'd take some convincing, and Standish, your father, said more than that. He said to remind you that he used to call you MJ, or Tappit Hen. Something about your fondness for port wine."

Startled, she backed away. Damn! She'd left a potential weapon--the heavy wine bottle--on the edge of the table. It was too far for her get to it, if he advanced. But...

"There are others who would know that," she hedged, but she grew surer by the moment.

Exasperated, the man added, "Standish said you have a birthmark on your inner thigh," he snapped. "It's shaped like a crown."

Shocked, she gaped. Only her father would be *gauche* enough to use *that* as an identifier! She wasn't sure Char knew it existed.

There was a noise from the hall and the irritation flared in his gaze. "Damn. Not enough time."

"You've come for the tray," she said briskly, and loudly, in English. "Now take it and go."

"Yes, Fräulein," he said, in the same rough German he'd spoken earlier when talking to the guard. He dropped his shoulders and limped heavily to the table, deliberately knocking the napkin and silverware to the floor. He was picking them up, and wiping the wooden floor when the guard poked his head in.

"Franz?" the guard called to him, ignoring Grace.

"Ja, I knocked over the stupid English tea," he groused in his guttural dialect, mopping at the floor with the napkin to clear the spilled tea.

The guard laughed and said something about clumsiness around beautiful women.

"Ja." The man, Franz, picked up the large tray as if it weighed nothing. His posture remained stooped and painful as he turned to go. The stoop made him appear bulky and heavy, rather than tall and lean. How did he do that?

"*Gute Nacht*, Fräulein," he said, bowing over the tray, and, while his back blocked the guard's view, he gave her a saucy wink.

"*Gute Nacht*," she managed. What the hell was going on? Was he a rescuer or more danger?

Hand at her throat, clutching her secreted brooch, she watched them leave. The guard nodded, but there was a gleam in his eye she did not like. Not one bit. As a businesswoman, one learned to distinguish appropriate interest from that which was not.

This was not.

The guard was an obvious foe. But...did she now have an ally?

The door closed and locked, and Grace rubbed her hands up and down her arms to settle the goose bumps. This was a dangerous dance. The newly stoked fire blazed up and she moved closer, finally feeling warm.

The encounter was bizarre. Who was Franz? Was he really from Char? He was no manservant, or gardener, or huntsman, that was certain.

She looked at the table, and froze. The bottle now sat in the exact center of the table. She'd set it down near the edge, in the clear space beyond the tray. She had kept the bottle and glass, and not only as a potential weapon. She'd wanted a glass of wine before bed. Sleep wasn't easy to come by when you were a captive, and the wine helped. A little.

Slowly, carefully, she lifted the bottle. Had he left a note?

Beneath the dark green glass something glittered,

despite the low light. A ring had been positioned to exactly fit where the deeply indented punt at the bottom of the bottle would hide it.

Not just any ring.

It was hers. The last time she'd seen it, it had been in the vault at Dale Manor, their country estate. Her father lived in London most of the year, as did Char. Someone would have had to have gotten the ring from the country house for a very specific purpose.

"Or it's been stolen," she muttered to herself, not believing it, even as she said it. Stealing the gem, only to bring it here, would be too complex a plot, even for her suspicious mind.

She slipped it on. The fifteenth century gem, set in gold, slipped on easily. Originally a man's signet ring, it was one of her favorites, and had been since she was a child.

The American really was a messenger from Char and her father. This, and knowledge of the birthmark, were enough proof.

Hitler would arrive within twenty-four hours. That changed the game, and the security situation. Her new American ally needed to strike now and get her out.

She was still pondering it as she dressed for bed an hour later. There were enough sheets to tie together to get her down from the second story window. The bed was heavy enough to use as a tie-off.

She was still eyeing it when there was a tap on the glass of the second story window.

CHAPTER THREE

Grace spun in place and stared. There at the window, motioning impatiently for her to let him in, was the manservant, Franz.

What in God's name?

She reacted instantly and raced to open the large casements to allow him to enter. A part of her considered leaving him hanging on the window ledge, by whatever contrivance he'd gotten himself there. But he'd proved his *bona fides*. She had to trust him.

Dressed in all black, his face soot-covered and darkened, he quickly pulled the ropes he'd used to rappel down from the roof off to one side, securing them in the ivy. He shut the windows quickly, and pulled the curtains.

The scars looked worse, somehow, covered in the concealing coal dust. Now, there was no eye patch to obscure that the accident, whatever it was, had transected, but miraculously hadn't taken, the eye. Both piercing, nearly-black eyes met her gaze, and once again, he winked.

Putting a finger to his lips, he walked to the door, neatly avoiding a creaky board as he did. He pressed his ear to the crack between the door and jamb, listening for the guard.

He nodded, and turned back to her. The look in his eyes was appreciative, but he quickly looked away.

"Get a robe, will you?" he said.

She'd forgotten her state of undress in her haste to get him in, unseen. Blushing, she snatched the robe she'd put on the foot of the bed and belted it on.

"Who are you, really?" she said, infusing her voice with ice.

"Shhh," he shushed her, easily dropping to the floor as she had, to peer under the crack. "Gregor is still out there," he whispered when he stood back up.

"Gregor?"

"The guard. We have to keep our voices down, unless you've become known for talking to yourself."

"I most certainly have not," she defended in a near-voiceless whisper.

He moved impossibly close, speaking as quietly as she had.

"My name's Robert Dixon. Call me Dix. I'm an American, as you guessed. I'm a friend of your brother's and I know your father, as I work for him at the Home Office. Sort of," he said the last with a quirky grin. "I'm here to get you out."

A dozen emotions ran through her mind, but she zeroed in on the one she most needed. Closing her eyes, she let go the first, immediate, swell of irritation and fury she'd felt for him, and for his winking, high-handed attitude.

"Thank you."

He looked surprised. "That's it?"

"Yes. Am I annoyed that my superiors think I can't get out of this on my own? Of course." She dismissed that with a wave of her hand, an unconscious mimic of her father's habitual gesture. "But not so much that I won't take help. Especially in the face of Herr Hitler's arrival."

She gave him a minute scan, noting the weapons scattered over his person, as well as the husky physique she'd noted--and reluctantly admired--earlier. "I'm glad you're armed. I'm not."

"Necessary, I assure you. They're expecting those important guests, including *der Führer*, as you say. It's getting busy around here. We have to get out while we can. Tonight."

"Yes. Most definitely," she agreed. "I can't leave until I get the diary back, however." She turned to the wardrobe, pulled out trousers and boots, preparatory to dressing for the hike they were going to take. "It's in the Library, or was. We have to get that first."

"Diary?"

"Family heirloom," she offered that excuse. She didn't know this man. Even if he worked for her father, he could still have Nazi sympathies, or not be as close-mouthed as someone needed to be, given the information she'd written in the book.

Before he could say another word, there were voices in the hall.

"Someone's coming," he hissed. "Where can I hide?"

"Under the bed," she said, "Quickly!" She shoved the clothes into the wardrobe, and motioned for him to roll under the high, old fashioned four poster. A half-a-dozen people and their children could hide under that wide expanse, much less one big American.

"No way. Where else?" he said, in a flat, hissed whisper.

"That's it," she replied, furious and afraid as the voices came closer. "The wardrobe is barely deep enough for a coat. The curtains are too obvious, you'd be easily seen. The bed or nothing," she insisted, shoving at his shoulder to make him drop to the floor.

"Dammit," he cursed, startling her with his vehemence. "Just my luck."

With reluctant speed, Dix dropped and rolled under the bed. She smoothed the fabric skirting on the side of the bed, and hurried to be sure she'd secured the latch on the window.

A knock sounded and the key immediately turned in the lock.

"Fräulein?"

"Here," she said, recognizing the matronly voice of the housekeeper. She'd hastily dropped onto the settee near the fire, pulled the blanket up to cover her feet, and snatched her book up as she did. "I was about to get ready for bed, Frau Shemper. What do you need?"

"Oh! I'm sorry to disturb you. I brought the warming pan." The older woman easily hefted the brass pan filled with coals, flipping back the coverlet and sheeting to glide the pan over the cool linen sheets to warm them. "It will be very cold tonight, and there will be snow. Also, I am wanting to let you know that our Führer will be here by lunch time. This is unexpected, and early, yes?" She beamed, and flipped the blankets over the warming pan.

"So," she continued. "I will press your good day clothes for you tonight, ja?" She bustled to the wardrobe, pulling it open and taking out two day dresses, a skirt and a crisp, finely woven cotton and silk blouse. "These I will press, in case you need to change or we are to go in the garden to meet our Führer when he arrives, ja? So, I will say good night." She frowned into the wardrobe for a moment then shut the door. She motioned to the bottle of wine. "Do you need a new glass, Fräulein?"

The glass on the table lay on its side, dripping one lone drop of wine from its rim. It had evidently fallen over, or been knocked over when Dix entered the room.

"Oh, for goodness sake," Grace exclaimed as she leapt from her sitting place to right the glass. "I didn't realize I'd turned it over. I'm sorry, Frau Shemper, I have stained the table linen."

"Ah, not to worry, Fräulein," Frau Shemper soothed, her frown fading as Grace wiped at the floor with a lace edged handkerchief pulled from her sleeve. She hated to ruin the fine linen and lace, but didn't want the woman to get down on the floor herself and possibly see Dix.

"Oh, nein, nein," she protested, hurrying to pluck the cloth from Grace's hands. "I should have done that," the housekeeper scolded. "Or have been sending Franz to do it. Here, let me take that." The housekeeper held the stained lace well away from the garments she'd laid over her arm and tsk-ed over the state of the white linen and lace, liberally stained with red wine. "I will see to it, I have much that I can do to take out the wine. Do you want a new glass?"

"No, no, I'm fine," Grace said, and corked the

bottle with ease. Thank goodness the bottle, three-quarters full of red wine, hadn't turned over as well. "I was about to go to bed."

The housekeeper nodded. The stained square of the handkerchief disappeared into one of Frau Shemper's skirt pockets.

"Yes, I was afraid I might wake you." Frau Shemper set the clothing aside long enough to collect the warming pan. She neatly flipped the covers into place, then, without the slightest bobble in the pan, she gathered the garments and bobbed a curtsey. "I'll see to these and have them for you in the morning."

"Thank you, Frau Shemper. Good night." Grace ushered the woman to the door, holding it as the housekeeper stepped into the hall.

"Good night, Fräulein." The woman bobbed a curtsey and pulled the door to. Housekeeper and clothing vanished in a wave of cold air from the hall as the door shut with a snap. The guard turned the key and Grace was alone.

Well, almost.

Damn. The timeline was now a ticking clock. She had to find the diary before Hitler arrived, and get out of the manor house before security increased exponentially with his presence.

"Dix?" she whispered. "You can come out. She's gone."

She heard the muted rustle of fabric, and Dix scooted out from under the bed. He lay on the floor, immobile, breathing heavily.

"What's wrong?" she demanded, kneeling to check his pulse. His skin was clammy with sweat and his heartbeat bumped at an erratic pace.

"Nothing," he muttered, pulling his wrist from her

grasp. "Give me a minute."

"You're sweating. Your heart rate is irregular. You're not all right," she said flatly.

"No, but I will be," he said, his whisper harsh in the dusky room. "Now leave it."

Offended at having her concern shoved in her face, Grace stalked to the window, giving him the space he'd so rudely requested. Within a few minutes, he rose. His breathing had moderated to normal, and he was again careful to make no sound. As annoyed as she was, she was intrigued with him. How could such a big man move so quickly? So silently?

"That diary isn't worth your life," he said, his whisper sharp.

She shook her head, then, realizing he might not see that in the dim light, she gripped his shoulder, and pulled him down to her so she could speak clearly.

"You misunderstand, Mr. Dixon. It isn't a simple heirloom. It's a valuable business tool. It can't fall into the wrong hands."

How to make him understand without telling him all?

"I have notes in it that I need for Char and my father."

He shook his head in disbelief. "They said you were smart. Canny. It doesn't matter." He dismissed her excuses. "No matter how important you think it is, my job is to get you out, not go chasing after some book and get us both caught." Dix opened the wardrobe and gestured. "Get dressed."

He also pulled out the soft suitcase on the floor of the cabinet.

"Pack a few things, and let's go."

Grace backed away. She had no sure way to know

if this man, this Dix Dixon was legitimately from her brother, despite the comment about the birthmark. The ring was convincing. But if he was, Char would have known to tell him--or her father would have--that she wouldn't leave without the diary.

"No."

He whipped around, his face a study in shock. "What do you mean, no?"

"Just that. I won't go without the diary."

"You will," he hissed, walking towards her. There was a menace in his face now that hadn't been there before. "I have a job to do and you're it. I don't go back on my word, and I don't fail. If I have to tie you up, gag you and haul you kicking and thrashing over the border, it will be hard, but I'll do it."

To her chagrin, Grace retreated a step. She wanted to stand firm, but in the face of this grim man, she felt a trickle of unease.

He meant it.

"I believe you," she said. And she did. "But that diary is worth more than my life and yours put together."

His expression implacable, he advanced, then, unaccountably, he stopped.

She'd seen a wolf once, in Russia. The massive creature had stopped, silent and powerful, a picture of contained violence and play in one creature. She remembered it standing, as Dix now stood, head cocked ever so slightly, listening.

His sharp jawline and prominent cheekbones were limned by the light from the fireplace, making him an icon carved from some dark, rich wood. The attraction she'd felt sneaking around the edges of her consciousness blew through her, full force.

Her belly constricted, and she felt every inch of her femininity as she pressed her knees together to keep them from wobbling. Here was the pack leader. The alpha wolf.

"They're here, the advance guards. Damn," he cursed harshly. "I'll be back, and diary or no diary, I will get you out of here."

She still hadn't heard whatever had alerted him. She strained to catch any sound other than their harsh, entrained breathing.

"Not without the diary." She managed to keep her voice firm. Implacable.

He was at the window before she saw him move. "Your brother and father would skin me alive for letting a book keep me from bringing you home."

Now, finally, she heard what he'd heard. The roar of powerful engines in the distance, then, the grind of truck gears.

Troop transports, most likely. Hitler's advance guards.

He pulled the ropes close to the window, slid out the casement ready to climb upward.

She had to make him understand. From the determined set of his jaw, he would do as he said and take her, willing or unwilling. She had to make him understand. She couldn't leave without the diary.

He rested a booted foot on the sill, and looked upward as he prepared to climb.

"Be ready," he hissed. It was all he said.

She leaned out, decision made. She had to trust him. Her gut said he was dangerous, her body wanted him, and her mind argued there was still a remote chance he was a Nazi spy.

Head or gut?

Which was right? Were they both right?

It didn't matter. She was out of time.

"Dix," she said, restraining him. He looked down, impatient to start the upward climb. "My brother and father would kill me themselves if the codes and ciphers in that book fall into Hitler's hands."

His face betrayed his shock. "You're joking."

"Not in the slightest," she declared. "It's far more important than my life. If you have to, and you can get the book, leave me and take it, get it back to London. That's how it needs to be."

The surprise on his face was the last thing she saw before the headlights from the trucks lit the road, and raised a shout from the guards at the gate.

CHAPTER FOUR

There was a bustle of activity as the trucks rolled up to the gates and were passed through.

Grace hastily shut the window, but left it unlocked. If Dix could get the book and get her tonight, they could go.

If not...

She tugged at the belt on her robe, and paced to the wardrobe, the floor creaking beneath her feet. She stopped. How had he moved so quietly? How had he known the creaking board was there?

It was as if he was that wolf she'd envisioned.

She shivered at the thought, and warmed herself again at the hearth. The flames were mesmerizing. Watching them let her put everything aside and think.

First things first. She should set up her bag so she could grab it and go. If there was no time for the bag, she needed to be dressed as warmly as possible at all times so if she had to go in what she stood in, she could.

That might be challenging if he didn't get her

before dinner tomorrow. Grace shuddered at the thought of coming face to face with the maniac who had ordered the invasion of Poland and caused her own beloved England to declare war.

The rumors about his changes in Germany were horrifying. Especially the reports that he championed active eugenics—-the segregation and isolation of non-Germans and those he considered defectives into specific areas and neighborhoods. The darker rumors said there were hospitals where the ill or troubled went in, but never came out.

His *Volkstum* prattle of a folksy, happy countryside, focused on a *pure Germany* as his propaganda put it. Other rumors had come from her connections, as well, rumors of old people and orphans being rounded up and sent away. They too were never heard from again.

Rumors aside, it was obvious the man was ruthless and power-mad. Those who foolishly dismissed his influence after the *Bierkeller Putsch,* a coup attempt, which came a mere two years after the Armistice, which ended the Great War, were no longer laughing.

Most were no longer living.

And stories of his abiding interest in the occult were now common knowledge on every continent.

Grace clutched the brooch. Oh, Lord in heaven. Was that it?

She'd never experienced the jewel's power. Although she'd had suitors and been engaged once, no one had yet brought out the supposed power of the gem. Aunt Grace had insisted most emphatically that she would know. It was Aunt Grace who'd convinced her to end her engagement.

"The quality of the dream will tell you the jewel is

at work," her Lady Aunt had assured her with a dreamy smile. "But don't trust the literal vision," she had warned. "It will fool you, and frustrate you, but you'll know you're on the right track when you begin to have the dreams."

Her fiancé had elicited no dreams, and no real spark of love either. With Aunt Grace's help, she'd ended it before it had hardly begun.

"Right then," she said, shaking off the memory. "That's not going to happen, in Germany, on the brink of war," she reassured herself. "That's for home and hearth. And, since its likely pure bosh as well, I'm setting it aside. Time for action, not dreams."

The legend of the jewel, and destined love, made for a good story. That, evidently, is what got her stuck here. No wonder General Freisenstadt hadn't questioned her about her travels. It had been the book, yes, but not for her codes. Hitler wanted the jewel.

Now that it made sense, Grace's determination settled in. She eased the wardrobe open. From the drawers at the bottom of the gorgeous old mahogany cabinet she took underthings, silk stockings and shoes, then slipped them in the bag. She left several pairs as well, rearranging and fluffing them to make the drawers look full.

There were notes and papers in the bag tucked under the false bottom. Frau Shemper hadn't found them, and until now, Grace had left them there, not wanting to call attention to her bag or anything else. They were valuable documents, but she could remember most, if not all of the information they contained.

If she could take them with her, all the better. If not, she would toss them in the fire and be sure they burned before she left.

Done with all she could do tonight, Grace banked the fire and hurried to get under the covers. The huge, solid bed was comfortable. It's down filled coverlet and linen sheets lay heavy on her shoulders as she snuggled into the pillows. She had a last wistful thought of home and her own heavily curtained bed before sleep claimed her.

The dreams came swiftly.

Bold colors swirled in her mind, making her smile in her sleep. They were so bright! Nothing like her usual dreams.

The images settled into place with a snap, however, and she saw herself, hand in hand with a German officer. The braid and silver buttons, the insignia and sharply outlined red swastika on the black wool of his coat declared his superior rank, he was one of the elite Nazi faithful.

Most of his face was shadowed by his stiff uniform cap, but his lips twisted in a harsh smile as he pulled her along behind him.

In her big, wide bed, desperately trying to wake up, Grace held onto the jewel like a lifeline. The gold was cold now, as cold as the snow in the vision's winter night.

The dream ended as abruptly as it began, with him dragging her out of the door of a small building, into the darkest of nights, into the blowing snow. The door closed behind them with an audible *snap*, shutting out the last gram of warmth and peace in her soul. Her heart pounded in fear, hammering like it would leap out of her chest.

Grace jolted awake, and sat bolt upright in the bed, gasping, one hand clutching the jewel, the other pressed to her galloping heart. The jewel was a heavy, reassuring warmth in her hand, helping to calm and soothe her spirit.

The dream. It flooded into her waking consciousness in bright, vivid detail.

It hadn't been like other dreams.

Is *this* what her Aunt had meant about the visions that came with the jewel? Had this horror, this nightmare, showed her intended, destined husband?

A Nazi? Oh, dear God.

Worse, a *Schutzstaffel* officer?

German and Nazi were bad enough, but the SS? They were at the heart of every evil, horrid rumor coming from Germany for more than a decade.

Dear Lord, what can I do?

In the gardener's quarters, Dix fumed. If she'd just come with him they could be halfway to the border. Instead, he was stuck trying to find a stupid book.

He loved books, but no book, including one with ciphers and codes, was worth a life.

He'd changed clothes on the roof, then slipped down the back wall of the lodge, walked the steep rooftree of the kitchen annex, and climbed down the ancient, wide branches of the snow-covered elm growing there.

"Mysteries, secrets," he muttered in his father's native Cherokee. "A woman who protects both."

He wanted to curse her for her stubbornness, as he simultaneously admired her wit and courage. If she was a courier and the secrets were kept in the diary she'd spoken of, then she was far more than she seemed.

She was also in one hell of a dangerous position.

The troops coming in--soldiers who'd nearly spotted him as he'd exited her room--were added guards for the compound in advance of Hitler's arrival the next evening. After the attempt on his life earlier in the summer, Hitler took no chances with his safety.

Two additional cars had driven in advance of the truck, and those held several more high ranking officers and their *aides de camp*.

Grace and her book might be a small part of this, but this was a meeting for other things. Major things.

Dix frowned. How could he get in to hear what was going on? There was a root cellar, part of which extended under the dining room. There was a dumb waiter to send up wines, ciders and casks of regional beer, which were kept in the cool of the cellar. The problem was, he wasn't kitchen staff.

He was a gardener-slash-woodsman-slash-manservant. He'd gotten the post by bribing the man who'd been in the position with passage to England. It was a dangerous, expensive bribe. He couldn't be sure the man would actually take the ticket and go, or whether he would turn Dix in. He thought he'd read his man right, but...

It wouldn't have mattered if they could have left tonight. There was no way the man could make it back here to report Dix to anyone, not from where Dix had left him. The longer Dix stayed, however, if the man was planning a double cross, the higher the chance that Dix would be caught.

Also, the more he interacted with people, the more

difficult it was not to slip up and betray his American origins. He'd managed to stay out of sight of the German military as he'd made his way to Zweiburg. The obvious stoop and limp he'd employed, with the eye patch and scars on his cheek, he was believable as a damaged, lowly workingman going to take his cousin's place at the hunting lodge.

He'd already been told that he wouldn't be allowed in the house when Hitler was in residence. Hitler despised damaged people. Although Dix's alter-ego, Franz, claimed his injuries came from serving in the Great War, Frau Shemper told him to stay out of Hitler's sight.

Hitler wanted only perfect Germans.

"Wonder if he knows how much his perfect German generals hate him?" Dix muttered, still using the Cherokee language as he coiled the climbing ropes into tidy bundles.

He rolled himself into a blanket and settled by the fire to sleep, intending to rise a little before dawn. He woke with a start and a feeling of deep unease, however, after only a few hours' sleep.

Lady Grace Corvedale. She'd been in his dreams. She was in danger. He stood up, but forced himself to stop.

To think.

The dream feeling wasn't now. It wasn't this minute.

Dix shivered in the cold room, and quickly stirred up the fire. Gardener's cottages, like the drafty upper stories of the lodge, didn't rate the centralized heaters that warmed the downstairs rooms.

Finally, when he'd warmed up and the haunted feeling had dissipated, he composed a message. He wrote it out first, then encoded it onto a fine, thin scroll of paper.

Queen of Hearts at the top of the deck. True Knight is feeling the Jester. She must have her tome or never travel. Ace of Spades arrives. The deck is stacked against a fight. Keep options 4QZ375L open.

There. Best he could do.

Going to the dovecote, Dix took out one of the special pigeons he'd brought in the battered old truck he'd driven from Freyming-Merlbach. He kept both pigeons and truck out of sight. He didn't want these pigeons to get loose, nor have them made into pie. The truck he kept on a hunting track away from the lodge. It would, hopefully, be their way out.

He rolled the note into its special tube and attached it to the bird's leg. He stroked a gentle hand down the bird's back.

As dawn broke he slipped into the woods, listening for patrols or the creak of boots on the snow. An expert woodsman, Dix knew this was a vulnerable moment. He hadn't had enough time to get the measure of the new troops. He didn't know their routines, because they hadn't established them.

The chaos of that was opportunity for failure.

Whispering to the bird in Cherokee, he tucked it into his coat. Taking up a rabbit gun, a roll of twine and a game bag, he boldly left the cottage and headed into the woods. He waved to one of the guards, but since he was heading away from the house, the man simply waved back and let him go.

One hurdle cleared. Once into the woods, with the day brightening, he felt almost cheerful. He gave it more than an hour's walk before he considered letting the pigeon fly. With Franz's limping gait, an hour hadn't actually taken him as far away as he wanted.

He'd have to risk it. He didn't want to be gone too long. At the edge of a clearing, he stopped to listen, his posture that of the gardener, but his senses fully alert and aware in the quiet stillness. Nothing stirred.

Finally, he straightened and brought the pigeon out from under his coat. Thurrring to it softly, he said the words that would send it winging to Standish, or, more likely, Shippingston.

"Go home, Rosie. Go home."

With a heave, he tossed the bird into the air, tensed for a shot or a shout. He didn't relax until the bird's wings caught the wind. It circled a moment, the headed west. Dix dared to stand a bit taller and watch the bird streak away. Toward the coast. Toward London.

"Strong wings, strong heart, good flight to you Rosie-bird," he muttered, returning to the gardener's stoop and shuffle, to make his way back through the snow. As he went, he stopped to gather branches of both holly and fir. Frau Shemper was fiercely Lutheran, but she kept the pagan tradition of holly and ivy at the doors and hearth at Yuletide.

With the generals coming, she'd demanded mistletoe as well, if he could find it.

Though he doubted it made an appearance in the main rooms, there was an advent ring in the kitchens with two wicks already charred as the season progressed. With no children in the house, there was no need for presents, or talk of the *Christkindl*, but he'd heard both Frau Shemper and the cook, Frau Krakle, humming carols as they worked.

"I wonder what Hitler will make of that," he muttered. As to mistletoe, Dix knew where to look, and soon found a great-grandfather oak.

He was gazing up at it when he felt eyes on him. He let his back stoop a little more as he used his hatchet to mark a blaze on the lodge-side of the tree.

"Ho, you there!" a voice shouted. "What are you doing?"

There was the crunch of booted feet on the snow and two of the new, and heavily armed, soldiers slogged their way to him. Had he been standing properly, he would have towered over them. Stooped as he was, he came only to their shoulders.

He answered in the guttural German dialect he's adopted for Franz.

"Eh, what about? I'm gittin' yon mistletoe fer Frau Shemper, belike she wants it quickish."

The younger man nodded and relaxed but the other didn't.

"What did he say?" The older man demanded of the younger.

"Ah, lay off, Carl," the younger soldier grinned at Dix, inviting him to share the joke of miscommunication on the older man. "He's just country-like. Getting' mistletoe for the housekeeper."

Both men grinned. Catching one of the housemaids under the mistletoe was totally acceptable in a country house, so it would only benefit them.

"I're gots te get a ladder belike," Dix muttered, pointing upwards. "Found it, gotter get it."

The younger soldier squinted upward in the early morning light. "Aye, sir, I can get that for you. No ladder needed. Here." He handed Dix his rifle, and stripped off his coat, which he handed to his comrade. "This'uns easy to climb."

Within minutes, the young man climbed up into the high branches of the oak and used a pocketknife to cut loose a heap of mistletoe.

Dix bobbed his head toward the young man. "Thenkee, young'un. It'd a taken me a bit o' time for that, e'en with the ladder. You saved me a mort o' work."

"No problem, sir," the youngster said, buttoning his coat. He took a sprig of mistletoe from the bunch and tucked it into the buttonhole at the top of his coat. "There. I'm well paid. Never know, right?" he said, grinning at the other two men. The older soldier, Carl, bent and broke off a sprig as well, agreeing that it was payment in plenty.

They shared cigarettes and quiet in the woods as Dix lashed the bundle of prickly mistletoe to the mess of holly and pine branches he was bringing back for Frau Shemper. When he was done, he and the men walked companionably back to the house in the brightening day.

"Frau Krakle has breakfast," Dix growled the words, but grinned at the men from his stooped position. "Her'n sausages are best 'round these parts. Puts 'em up herself, belike."

The men--the younger more of a boy than a man--grinned.

"Good duty this, eh?" Carl commented. "If the food's always as good as it was when we came in last night."

He slapped Dix on the shoulder hard enough to make him wince, and tromped toward the kitchen entrance. The younger man grinned again, and offered a hand to help tow the mass of greens to the kitchen door.

"Thenkee for yer help," Dix said, smiling in return.

"Of course. Gave me a chance to get this, ja?" The boy pointed to the sprig of mistletoe. "That'll get me a kiss or two. Early present from the *Weihnachtsmann.*"

Dix laughed and agreed that Father Christmas was more likely to enjoy those kind of gifts than the more angelic *Christkindl.*

They were sharing a last smoke when Dix once more caught the roar of a powerful engine. He pretended not to notice until there was a shout and a cheer. Pulling up to the gate was a motorcade, flagged and bedecked with swastikas.

Der Führer had arrived.

CHAPTER FIVE

From her window, Grace watched the most powerful man in Germany--perhaps in all of Europe at the moment--exit his car. She'd cracked the window open slightly so she could hear.

A man in the detested grey and black Nazi uniform opened the passenger door rather than the back, much to her surprise. Alighting from the elegant Mercedes, Adolf Hitler took in a deep breath and smiled.

"Ah, the air is so good in Germany," he remarked. Turning, he smiled at the tall man who'd opened his door. "Thank you, Kempka." The chauffer bowed slightly, snapping his heels together as Hitler surveyed the lodge. Grace froze in place. Even knowing she couldn't be seen, the power of the man's gaze surprised her.

He wasn't the man from her dream. That man had been tall, his chin a sharply chiseled line. Hitler's chin was rounded, his shoulders slightly stooped. The chauffer was tall, but not the right build, though he was an officer.

"You don't believe in it," she muttered desperately. "Why does it matter?"

She just needed the book.

The sound of hurried footsteps on the outer stairs had her racing for the bed. She yanked up the covers and, as the door swung open, sat up as if she'd been disturbed from deep sleep.

"What is it?" She shielded her eyes from the oil lamp Frau Shemper carried on a large tea tray. It was a dark, gloomy day and not far along into the morning. The oil lamp cast bright light, but also made heavy shadows in the curtained, west-facing room.

"Fräulein, he is here!" Frau Shemper exulted. "Come, come, you must dress. He wants to meet with you immediately. I've brought you tea," she said unnecessarily, setting the tray on the table.

The housekeeper hurried to stir the fire's embers and to throw on one of the dwindling supply of logs. The old lodge had been electrified on the main floor, but not in the upper rooms.

Here, evidently, one was expected to make do with oil lamps and the fireplace. This was, after all, supposed to be a rustic retreat for gentlemen taking weekends to hunt and fish, away from city concerns, not a pampering hotel with full electric and gas laid on.

"Franz is bringing water for you to wash. We will have the boiler up later, before dinner, and you may take a proper bath in the new lavatory, but for now, you will freshen up, ja?"

Frau Shemper didn't wait for her to answer as she turned to berate Franz as he made his silent way in the door. "Hurry up, you lazy fool. She must go down within the hour."

Franz grunted in reply, setting down a large, covered copper footbath. Grace hadn't seen it's like since she was a child, and then only at the country estate. In the barn.

"Water," he said, turning to leave.

"*Nein, nein*," Frau Shemper said. "You see to the fire while I get her clothes. Wilhelm," she called out, firing off orders as she left. A younger man had replaced Gregor. He peeked in the door, blushing when he saw Grace by the bed. He promptly turned his face to the hallway. Although the light was low, she saw that the tips of his ears were bright red from his blush.

Stupid to turn your back.

"Green," Dix muttered, shooting her a look from the one dark eye not covered by the tatty black patch. He nodded toward the young guard.

Evidently he'd seen her look and calculated its meaning. She allowed a brief smile and his flashed in return.

Dix loaded in another log and watched it catch. He wished the flue in his hunting cabin back home drew this well.

A different kind of hunting, here in Germany.

"Are you packed?" he said, under the cover of pulling the fire screen back into place.

"As ready as I can be without the book," Grace murmured.

"If you get it, put something white at the window glass, I'll come for you."

Before she could answer, Frau Shemper bustled in again, Grace's neatly pressed garments in her arms.

"Shoo, shoo," she said, flapping at the men, who retreated, closing the door. "Here now, Fräulein. This nice wool, ja? And the jacket."

The beautiful blouse was crisp with pressing and a light starch, and her wool suit was pressed to a perfect smoothness. If she'd been at home, she'd have been delighted.

"Thank you Frau Shemper. When should I be ready?"

"Three quarters of an hour," Frau Shemper said, approval in her voice. "I'll come for you."

With that, the woman bustled out, leaving Grace to decide between tea and wash water.

"Tea." Nothing should come before a bracing cup of tea. In the face of dictators and magical dreams, she needed it strong. She stirred sugar in, added milk and tested it for taste.

"Perfect." How ironic that tea in France had been an ordeal to get prepared correctly, and her hostile captors made it to English exactitude.

Grace took advantage of the water while it was still somewhat hot, then dressed, finishing the pot of tea and the tiny biscuits with ham along the way. She was buckling her stylish, but sturdy shoes when she heard the distinct sound of Frau Shemper's return. There were others with her, at least two by the sound of the boot steps.

This time when Frau Shemper knocked, she waited for Grace to invite her to enter before she unlocked the door. The older woman was still beaming, but she pushed open the door and motioned for Grace to come out.

"Herr General, may I present Lady Grace Corvedale?" Frau Shemper said in clear German. To

Grace, she added, in English, "Lady Corvedale, this is Herr General Vicktor Von Manselm, he will escort you to our wonderful leader."

Frau Shemper bowed to the man, and continued to beam and flutter as General Von Manselm snapped his heels together and bowed.

"Lady Corvedale, it is an honor to meet you. If you will come with me?" Von Manselm extended his arm for Grace to take. As an escort he was apparently perfect, in that he, like Frau Shemper, spoke impeccable English.

"*Danke*, General," she managed as she forced a pleasant smile to her face. "You speak English well, did you study abroad?"

"I did, Lady Corvedale. I took my degree at Trinity College, Oxford."

"Very good," she remarked. "And did you enjoy our fair island?"

"Very much," Von Manselm replied, covering her hand where it lay on her arm. "You'll want to watch the stairs, Lady Corvedale. The carpet is unsteady on several of the steps."

"Thank you," she said, infusing a chill into her voice. He removed his hand at once and they made their way down the stairs, turning away from the front doors toward the comfortable library down the hall.

"I'm glad you could visit with us," Von Manselm continued, as if nothing were amiss. "I understand you brought something of interest to the Führer." He smiled warmly down at her. "Thank you for that. The burdens of governance are great, so those of us who are devoted to him appreciate when he can find entertaining distractions in the midst of so much important work."

"Indeed." It was all Grace could think to say. Was this the officer from her dream? He wore no SS insignia, but she'd been told that some officers didn't, and that others gloried in it.

Oh dear. She surreptitiously scanned his features as they paused outside the library doors.

No, his jawline was too soft, and he had a large moustache. The man in the dream had been darker skinned, with sharp chin and jaw. He'd also been clean shaven.

The general knocked and the door was opened by a uniformed staffer. Several men stood at the fire or sat at the large library table. At its head, her precious journal lay on an archivist's cloth. Sitting at the table, with her the journal in front of him, was *der Führer* himself.

"Ah," he said, congenially, standing. "Come, come, don't linger in the doorway!"

Von Manselm led her straight to Hitler, coming to attention immediately and clicking his heels smartly for second bow as they arrived at the end of the table. All other conversation in the room stopped.

"*Mein Führer*, may I present your honored guest, Lady Grace Corvedale?"

Hitler took her hand, bowing over it in a courtly manner. "Welcome, Lady Grace. You are indeed as lovely as the reports I received about you indicated. Please, sit."

Von Manselm pulled out a chair for her and Grace sat, as Hitler resumed his chair.

"How are you finding your stay? The staff has looked after you well?" Hitler asked, and Von Manselm translated. She'd told Frau Shemper she didn't have much German. A lie, of course. Her

German wasn't perfect, but it would have gotten her by. In this case, better to not admit it.

"All is well, *danke*," she replied in halting German. "I thank you for translating, General Von Manselm," she added, returning to English. "My German is quite scant."

"Yes, yes," Hitler replied, beaming at her use of the language. It seemed to please him all out of proportion. "Now, tell me, Lady Corvedale, how your family came to have this fascinating book?"

Frau Shemper bustled in with coffee and tea, bustling right back out when one of the aides blocked her and took the cart, wheeling it off to one side. Within moments, a steaming cup of tea, fixed to her exact standard, was set at her elbow.

"*Danke.*" She ignored all the niggling implications of this, and bullied her way forward. "It is a book of love stories," she said, simpering a little. "Tales of true love, of course."

Let's see what he made of that. Hopefully, he'd dismiss it.

The hope was dashed aborning, as Hitler thumbed through to a marked page. "This ancestor of yours, here," he pointed, noting a dated passage. She couldn't tell if it was 1658 or 1568, but it was old. "He is noted in history books, even in Germany, as a soldier of great renown." He nodded to himself, running a short, stout finger down the page. "And he is both English and German, yes?"

Grace held her hand out for the book. For a tense moment, she and Hitler stared at one another. With the faintest smile, he handed her the diary.

Grace quickly read the passage, remembering it from her first read of the book five years ago when it came to her at eighteen.

"Yes, his mother was German. A countess, I believe. My lady ancestor did not want to marry him. Not at first."

Hitler mimicked her gesture, holding his hand out for the book. Reluctantly she returned it and his smile widened. He was enjoying the cat-and-mouse of this exchange.

"And yet, marry they did, and had," Hitler paused, consulting a sheaf of notes at the side of the soft cloth on which he'd laid the book. "Ten children? Yes, here it is. Ten children. All of whom lived to adulthood. All of whom were marriageable and made good marriages."

He consulted another page, and a neatly dressed man moved up to Hitler's right side with a set of notes. She had barely noticed this man, so unobtrusive was he. He'd been here all along, however. He'd greeted them when General Freisenstadt delivered her to the lodge. The little man returned to sit to the side. On the table next to him lay a copy of Debrett's.

"This indicates good stock," he said, waving the pages. "All good marriages. No deformities. The sons did well, the daughters married well." He made it a statement, so she didn't deny it as Von Manselm translated.

"Yes, our family has been fortunate."

"No, they are strong," Hitler enthused. "Their roots in the Fatherland give them strength. The combination with the English bloodlines is important. It links our nations." There was a fervent light in Hitler's eyes when he turned back to her. "This is the key, Fräulein Corvedale. Linking nations of pure blood, making nations strong. Eliminating the weak, the malformed. Yes, yes," he said, staring off for a moment. "This is key."

When he refocused, his snapping eyes were sharp, and his mouth firm. "Let me see the jewel."

"Jewel?"

"The jewel, Fräulein." He flicked his gaze to Von Manselm and she felt the general's hand clamp down onto her shoulder.

With reluctance, she tugged on the chain at her neck, pulling the gem-encrusted gold brooch out from under her blouse. Hitler snapped his fingers, holding out his hand.

Before she could pull it over her head, Von Manselm's hands were at her nape, unfastening the catch. Revulsion shot through her. The touch of his bare skin on her neck made her want to retch.

"*Danke*, Vicktor," Hitler said absently, taking the jewel into his hand. Another man, who had been standing by a small table by the window, brought a jeweler's loupe when Hitler snapped his fingers.

Saying nothing, Hitler put the loupe to his eye and began a minute examination of the brooch. Every whorl of every lotus blossom, every facet of the rubies and of the massive sapphire were studied in the heavy silence that blanketed the library.

"Magnificent. Egyptian work, no doubt of it," Hitler breathed, and he sighed like a man waking up from a dream as he laid the brooch on the soft cloth next to the book.

Once again he turned his gaze to her. "The book, and the story I have heard, say the brooch only works for one woman in a generation. Is this true?"

"As far as I know from the legend," Grace

answered truthfully. She'd never actually thought about it. "The wearer must keep it with her once the gem comes to her."

That was true, according to her Aunt Grace. Not only was it of immense value, but supposedly, if it was ever lost, very bad things would happen to whatever branch of the family held it in trust. So many generations had passed from that first woman to possess it, Grace had no idea how many of her cousins, near and distant, those *very bad things* might apply to if it was taken from her.

"Ah, I see. So it could not be passed from girl to girl, to find her ideal partner?" he asked, keen interest making him lean toward her, as if to compel an answer.

"No," she answered, forcing herself to be truthful. "Again, the legend says *bad things happen* if it leaves the designated daughter too soon."

"Hmmm, hmmm," Hitler hummed to himself. "So, you have had the dreams?"

Startled by the change in subject, Grace denied it.

"Not yet." She forced a shrug, and stuffed down the memory of the vivid images, and the panic that wanted to choke her at the thought. "The previous wearers," she indicated the journal, "said that once you meet the person of your destiny, then the dreams begin." She shrugged, forcing a simple, innocent smile. "Supposedly this is how you know. My Aunt, who passed the jewel to me, said the dreams are different enough that you know." She reached for the journal, but he moved it away. "The diary, if you'll read some of the entries, tells the girl not to take the images too literally. Sometimes the images are...metaphors," she finished carefully, for lack of a better word choice.

He peppered her with more questions. Sticking to the truth as much as she could, Grace weathered what amounted to an interrogation ranging from her personal sleeping habits--questions she haughtily did not answer--to which members of Hitler's staff she had met so far. He then circled back to what she knew of the diary.

The discussion had an insidious quality, Grace realized. The man was, at points, charming, affable and genuinely amusing, which could lull anyone, including Grace, into thinking he wasn't zeroed in on that which he wanted. Then a question from out of nowhere would come, spot on, to hammer at her and drag more information from her.

"I have allies in your country, you know," he said, in the most casual tone, after just having baited her about her loyalties to the crown, her actions in Paris, and her supposed flirting with the vintner she now suspected of reporting her. "Many of your countrymen support our righteous cause."

"Indeed, is that so?" she replied, as coolly as she could muster. With only tea to sustain her, she'd been answering his questions for several hours. Her voice cracked slightly and she cleared her throat.

Hitler eyed her and snapped his fingers. "Fresh tea for Fräulein Corvedale," he ordered. "And tell Frau Shemper to lay on lunch. I'm famished," he said with a laugh, patting his waistcoat. "You'll join us for lunch of course, Fräulein?"

It was an order, not a request, but she inclined her head as if she had the option to refuse. "Of course, sir. Thank you. It is a pleasure to be out of my rooms."

The dig, given that she was a prisoner, shot home, but Hitler simply smiled.

"Ah, yes, well, it is good for all of us to learn our limits, ja? And then, when we are asked to surpass them, well, we are able to do so. Come, let us go to lunch."

He stood, and everyone in the room jumped to attention. Grace remained seated.

Before Von Manselm could hoist her up, or do anything equally bourgeois, Hitler stepped to her side and snapped his heels together, giving the slightest of bows. "If I might have the pleasure of escorting you, Lady Corvedale?"

Von Manselm's shocked translation was unneeded, and Grace allowed Herr Hitler to take her hand and help her to rise. Von Manselm pulled out her chair and stepped smartly out of the way.

Before he could offer her his arm, however, she leaned over the table and took up the brooch.

"It's unwise, according to the legend, to let the brooch out of my sight," she said, refastening the chain around her neck. While she dared not touch the diary, she let the brooch, on its gold chain fall onto her blouse.

Everyone in the room froze, either horrified by her audacity, or eager to see her punishment.

Hitler paused a moment, and she saw a twinkle in his eye. He threw back his head and laughed.

"Of course, it must be so." With a smile he extended his arm, and together they made their way to the dining room for lunch.

Dix paced the gardener's quarters. Up three strides, back three, across one and a half strides, back the other way. The room wasn't large enough to let off the pent up tension that rode him like an iron coat.

He had gone out into the gardens, hoping to catch a glimpse of Grace, to find out where she was being questioned, only to be shooed away from the front of the lodge by the guards. The young man he'd met in the woods, who'd been guarding Grace's room this morning, hustled him around the corner of the lodge as two generals stepped out onto the front lawn to smoke and talk together in low, earnest tones.

"You don't want to be seen here, Franz," Wilhelm warned. "*Der Führer* is agin' folk who're beat up a little," the boy said, with an apologetic smile. "Wouldn't want you to get in trouble."

Dix dropped into Franz's tones with a mocked up growl. "I be's getting' in trouble fer not tendin' the grounds is what I will be," he said.

"Not for now you won't." The boy looked around to be sure no one was watching. "Here, take my smokes. Go stay warm by your fire. Stay out of sight."

Dix held the pack. It was full. The boy didn't like to smoke. He made a show of it to seem the manly sort, but if there were even four cigarettes missing, Dix would be surprised.

He brightened his tone a fraction, replying, "Thenkee, lad," he said, eyeing the pack with pretended delight. "I'll be doin' that."

"At least for the rest of the morning, ja?" Wilhelm stood straighter. "Now be off with you," he snapped, pushing at Dix's shoulder as another soldier rounded the corner of the lodge. There was surprise on Wilhelm's face and Dix wondered why.

He looked down at the heavy leather and wool coat he wore----serviceable and old, bought from one of the German underground who didn't support the new regime. That wasn't it. It was something else.

The eye patch? The scars were real, though the patch was not.

The other soldier shot him a menacing look. That one had bully written all over him, so Dix growled a few insults about young pups and minding their betters, and slouched away to his quarters behind the converted barn.

Kempka, Hitler's main chauffer, had commandeered the stable master's quarters in the garage, sending the lodge's old driver, Johan, to stay at his sister's in Zweiburg.

Dix reached the safety of his rooms, slamming the door, and making sure it locked. Only then did he straighten up, and from there, he started his fruitless pacing.

Finally, as late afternoon brought lowering clouds, he made up his mind on what to do. He resumed his coat and his limp, and trudged to the kitchen entrance.

"Town fer supplies," he growled, holding out a hand for Frau Krakle's list. She'd lamented that no one would go and get her supplies. Everyone wanted to be at the lodge and catch sight of the Führer and his staff.

Delighted, Frau Krakle waddled his way, thrusting a list and a wad of *Reichsmarks* into his hands. "*Danke*, Franz. You're a godsend. What would we have done with Klaus breaking his legs in that terrible accident? You're a good cousin to come take his place, despite your own injuries," she simpered at him, but her voice was a patronizing whine.

The woman took special pains to point out Franz's supposed injuries and infirmities, as she pretended to be in great sympathy with him. If he truly had been the former gardener's cousin, he wouldn't have stayed for a moment, the way the woman treated him.

As it was, he glared at her and stomped out to the garage. Bypassing the lounging soldiers, he started the lodge's big car and drove to the gate. It ran better now than when Dix had dropped Klaus, his mother, and two nieces at a remote spot on the French border with enough money for bribes, and passage to America for all of them.

Maybe by the time Dix returned from the village, there would be a signal in Grace's window.

CHAPTER SIX

By the time Grace returned to her rooms, mid afternoon, she was exhausted. All of the highest ranking *Gauleiters*, Hitler's highest ranking district commanders, had been introduced to her one by one over lunch. Hitler had expounded on the glory of their Germanic pedigrees. Nowhere was Hitler's keen interest in eugenics, in ethnic cleansing and the breeding of a new nation more evident than in his extolling of the "Clean clear pedigrees that any woman would be proud to extend."

What she hadn't known was how deeply effective the man's personal charisma could be. No matter how inured to it she thought she was, Hitler had sneaked in such plausible, honest insights, that several times she'd been lulled into agreeing with his theories.

And the more he had talked, the more the *Gauleiters,* especially the very married Joseph Goebbels, had eyed her like a ripe melon or a rare beefsteak. Each had decided they would be the one Hitler selected to take her to wife.

At least the single ones had. The married ones just wanted to bed her for *Führer and Fatherland!*

Horrible thought.

Grimacing, she flung herself onto the settee. The man, Hitler, was abominably dangerous. He could make the most horrific act sound plausible, surrounding it with facts one could easily agree to, then slipping in the unthinkable.

"Surely you agree, Fräulein," he had said, in the most reasonable tone. "That you would never want one of your precious children to suffer? You would never condemn a darling babe to which you'd given birth, to slavery, or to pain, would you?"

She'd agreed, of course, that she would not want that for any child.

"Then how is it wrong to let them gently go back to God, when they are born with terribly deformities, or are born from an unwholesome mix of bloodlines, eh?"

Subtly and insidiously, he'd hammered away at her. Keeping her equilibrium and agreeing enough to make him happy, while remembering who and what she was, had been as exhausting as walking uphill from London to Dale Manor, on foot, alone in the dead of winter.

"At this point, I'd willingly do that," she muttered, wishing for tea, or perhaps a real, full bath so she could wash away the feeling of corruption that settled like a sticky coat of mud on her mind.

She heard steps and straightened, sitting prim and upright on the edge of the settee. When Frau Shemper entered, her face was alight.

"Oh, Fräulein! How wonderful for you!" the woman enthused. "I'm so happy!"

Suddenly afraid, Grace rose. "About what are you happy, Frau Shemper?"

"Oh, the gentlemen tell me you'll be picking one of them as a husband before the week is out, yes! And if none suit, our wonderful *Führer* has offered to escort you to Berlin and let you choose from among his many unwed staff there."

Frau Shemper beamed as if this were the greatest gift that could be bestowed on womankind.

"He is too kind," Grace managed, through clenched teeth.

So that was the game.

He hoped to use the jewel to expose her to someone who would be her mate. Then marry her off and use her family, her position in English society, as leverage somehow.

"I have the boiler heating," Frau Shemper added, bustling once more to the wardrobe. "I've hung the lovely afternoon dress here, to keep the wrinkles out. General Von Manselm has asked to entertain you with a game of chess if you play."

"Unfortunately I don't," Grace lied easily. "Perhaps whist?"

"Cards?" Frau Shemper frowned with thunderous disapproval.

"I do not gamble, Frau Shemper," Grace added. "Merely engage in the strategy of the game."

"Ah," Frau Shemper made the noncommittal noise. "I will inform Herr General."

"Thank you."

Von Manselm. She repressed a shudder. That he had lined up first in an attempt to woo her was not a good omen. However, if this dream nonsense *was* real, she could take great relief in knowing it wasn't he who was her destined mate.

"Ja, good, good." Frau Shemper spoke again, jerking Grace back to the moment. "And I will press this for you as well," she said, frowning over the simple evening dress. It wasn't impressive on the hanger, but it was when she put it on. She had packed it for show, in case her bags were searched. It would have been less plausible to not have evening wear for when she met with her mythical brandy seller. "*Gauleiter* Deiteriche will be escorting you down for dinner."

Good gad, was she to be trotted out like a brood mare every hour on the hour for a new stud?

Evidently so, as Frau Shemper hurried to tell her that a senior general, this one from the recently renationalized Saarlands district, would like to have an hour of her time discussing music over wine after dinner, and yet another would be here to fetch her for breakfast the next morning.

"Thank you Frau Shemper," Grace interrupted the flow of words, pressing a hand to her temple. "For the moment, I wish only to take you up on the offer of a bath, and perhaps I will lie down for a bit before cards."

"Yes, yes, of course." The older woman beamed once more and led the way to the bathing room, repositioning young Wilhelm outside the door. "When you are ready, Wilhelm will escort you back to your room."

"*Danke*, Frau Shemper."

Once she'd locked the door, Grace hurried to the small window. The narrow casement opened onto a steep, short roof. Closing her eyes to visualize the house, she realized this must overlook the kitchens, or some of the pantries. Shooting lodges often had extensive larders for the game, which was brought in from the hunt.

Beyond the kitchen, she saw a sizeable smokehouse and beyond that, the garages. Several men stood outside both buildings, smoking. Most had weapons slung over their shoulders.

Grace pulled the window closed. The vantage point was too vulnerable for escape, she decided. Too many of the loitering soldiers clustered at the garages--former stables with wide, treeless paddocks next to them--with no cover between the house and the trees to screen her from their view.

Off to the right, though, was a promising path. A walled garden, its vegetable plots now covered with straw and snow, offered considerable cover. On the far side a gate gave access to the woods. If the gate was locked, it appeared to still offer enough hand holds that she could climb it.

Grateful for the fine boiler, which heated the water to steaming perfection, she climbed into the bath. She'd piled her thick hair up, to keep it from the wet as she soaked.

With a sigh, knowing that time was flying by, Grace finally arose and pulled the plug on the generous claw-footed tub. Wrapping herself in a towel, she turned toward the foggy mirror, wiping it with a thick towel.

She drew breath to shriek when the cleared glass reflected not only her face but the sooty black of Robert Dixon's as well.

Dix's hand clamped over her mouth.

"Shhhhh," he murmured.

She nodded and he released her, stepping quickly

away. Grace clutched the towel firmly to her bosom. "What are you doing here?" she hissed. "If you're caught they'll shoot you on sight."

"*Der Führer* would like to do that anyway," Dix sneered, "Given that Franz is imperfect, scarred and deformed."

"Franz is--" Grace began hotly only to stop, remembering that Dix and Franz were the same man. "An illusion," she finished lamely.

"Yes. He is. There are servant's stairs," Dix said, looking at the tub, the ceiling, anywhere but at the luscious form of Grace Corvedale. "There are also tunnels."

"Tunnels?" Grace said eagerly, missing his shudder at the thought of being closed in, underground. With no light.

It won't be a problem. If it gets us out of Germany, I'll do it.

"How far do they go? Do they lead to the border?"

"I don't know yet. I just discovered their existence."

"The book," she began.

Dix held up a forestalling hand. "No time. I came to tell you to be ready tonight. Book or no book, we have to get out of here."

Her features set in a stubborn line. "I can't go without it, Mr. Dixon. Absolutely not."

"You have the necklace. You have the information in your head," he temporized. "We'll get the book if we can, but the longer you're here, the longer I'm here, the more danger we're in."

"It's not a necklace," Grace protested, letting go of the towel long enough to clutch the pendant. She hadn't taken it off, even in the bath. "It's a brooch. It's a family heirloom."

"And Hitler wants it," Dix said, flatly. "That alone is dangerous. Why?"

"Why what?"

"Why does he want it, and you?"

She avoided the question, saying, "I need to get dressed, go back to my room. I can't stay in here much longer."

"I know. Tell me about the brooch. It's obviously valuable for the gems alone." He gestured to the heavy gold and winking sapphire. "And you're wearing the ring."

When she tightened her hand around the ring, he grinned. "Standish thought you would recognize it. Does it stand as my *bona fides?*" he asked. "Do you finally believe me?"

"Yes," she acknowledged. Turning her back to him, she applied cream to her face, watching him through the mirror. "The ring is a family piece. My favorite."

"So's the brooch."

"Yes." She turned to the heavy robe she'd brought to the bathroom, slid her feet into the thick sheepskin slippers Frau Shemper had provided.

"Turn your back," she demanded. He did and there was a soft thud as the wet towel hit the floor. Part of him zeroed in on those elegant curves, and the memory of her standing in the cold bedroom in her nightgown, the sharp points of her nipples betraying her chilled state.

Stop that.

She was the sister of a friend, she was a member of the British upper class. He was an American, and a mongrel of that sort, as well.

And they were in peril. No time for admiring.

Or anything else.

"All right, you may turn around." There it was, he decided, that crisp diction, the accent, the ever-so-haughty tone. That was what he needed to keep his lusty reaction in check.

With an insolent grin, he turned. And stopped as attraction sucker-punched him right in the gut. Her hair framed her face in lush waves where it had come loose from the pins holding it up. The tightly belted robe highlighted more than it concealed, although she pulled the lapels across her generous breasts, it made little difference.

"What?" she said, looking over her shoulder for whatever he was staring at.

"Nothing. I hadn't seen you with your hair down."

She pushed at it.

"Leave it," he snapped, angry with himself for mentioning it. "I have to get out of here. Be ready. Tonight. After midnight."

"I'll be ready, but I won't go without the book."

He nodded. "You will if we have to," he corrected, "but we'll get it. Now," he said, moving to her, crowding her. He couldn't seem to help himself. She stood her ground at his approach, but he saw the awareness in her eyes and it fired something in him.

He bent down, so that his lips were at her ear. "You'll be safe with me," he murmured, careful not to touch her.

Her answer was low, but delivered crisply. The huskiness, however, told him all too well that she felt the pull between them. "I doubt that. Just get me out, Mr. Dixon."

He laughed, and tugged a lock of her hair. "Dix, sugar. Just Dix. And I will."

To her surprise, he stepped up on the seat of the loo and pushed open a hatch in the ceiling. She'd noticed it, but dismissed it for what it was, a way to check the old cistern should it be needed.

He pulled himself through the opening with one graceful movement, lifting his whole body through with the strength of his arms alone. How strong was he, to be able to do that?

To her surprise, he crouched in the attic space to look back at her.

"Midnight," he said with a grin, and was gone.

Talking with Hitler's generals was boring, Grace decided. The *Gauleiter* for Danzig, in the recently and forcibly captured Poland, was especially boring. Nevertheless, she listened attentively and carefully to Herr Forster.

She had gleaned a great many things during her stay, things the Home Office might find useful. For in their conversation, their clumsy wooing, they allowed the smallest bits of information to slip. To her great discomfort, Von Manselm lurked, watching her with hooded eyes, giving his rivals menacing stares as they too courted Grace.

By the time she was allowed to retire for the night, Grace was worn thin. Frau Shemper had brought a chocolate pot instead of tea, and a plate of small sandwiches. She pushed Grace toward the small table as she fluffed the bed and ran the warmer over the covers.

"There now, a bit of something for you. They've

had you talking and walking around the house for hours."

"Thank you, Frau Shemper. I admit, I'm famished." Grace took up the pot and poured out, adding a dainty ham sandwich to the little plate beside her saucer.

"Ja, well, it is all in a good cause. Soon you will choose one of our fine, fine generals." She beamed. There would be no persuading Frau Shemper to help her. The woman was smitten with Hitler and believed Grace could have no kinder, higher fate than to be married off to one of Hitler's top men.

Perhaps if she'd been German, or truly a guest, the matchmaking might have amused. In these circumstances, it did not.

"*Gute Nacht, Fräulein*! May you dream of your destined husband!" Frau Shemper said, bustling away with more clothes to press for the next day and a broad smile on her face.

As the lock ground into place, Grace shuddered and dropped into her chair with more relief than poise. Von Manselm was bad enough, as Forster had been. Boring, pompous, insufferable. General Hubert Schicth had been kind, in his way. That had almost been worse.

The man she's talked with last, Joseph Goebbels, was the worst by far. Though he was married, he had nonetheless flirted heavily with her. A short, stocky man, he had seemed taller due to the fervent passion that burned within him for Hitler's causes.

"Our leader has a great vision," he had declared, pressing two volumes into her hands as they left the library where he had insisted they sit. It had been hell to have the diary so close, and she was sure that he knew it. He had that sly edge to his word choice and way of speaking that told her he was baiting her with every word.

"You can see the beginnings here." He tapped the books that he'd closed into her hands, clasping his larger hands over hers and using his thumb to stroke her fingers. "We are to welcome you properly, see you settled in Germany, yes? The things you will learn from these great books, these humble books, are things to teach your children, Fräulein Corvedale. These are the things that will bring them glory in the new world order."

The books, a children's story, *Der Giftpilz*, and a novel, which glorified the *Wherbauer*, the German farmer-soldier, were the kind that simultaneously decried those of "subhuman bloodlines" such as gypsies, or Jews, while deifying the common German man.

Grace knocked them from the table. Poisonous mushrooms indeed! How insidiously was Hitler infecting the German people with this thought of racial unity?

"Werewolves, more than *Wherbauer*," she muttered, nudging the books with her foot.

Goebbels had indicated that he would be leaving in the morning for Berlin, going before Hitler, to prepare for her introduction to yet more of the Führer's generals. He slyly let her know that he too would be available to her, should she care to partake.

"It will be an icy day in hell," she snarled, galvanized by her revulsion. She quickly pulled the soft bag from the wardrobe and checked that the papers were undisturbed. The garments she'd put in the case had been returned to the drawers, but it was mere moments work to repack the bag with her warmest things. Dix said they were going to run, and run hard, straight for the border. France would give them refuge, and together she and Dix could make it to the coast.

At midnight, she was ready. She had on her heavy trousers and stout walking boots, all covered by a long, serviceable skirt, a sweater and the heavy canvas jacket she'd had for driving. All had been brushed or pressed and hung meticulously in the closet.

Now all that remained was for Dix to get the book, get her, and go.

The clock ticked away the minutes. At half-midnight, she began to pace, avoiding the creaking boards. By one, she finally sat, eating the last of the little sandwiches Frau Shemper had provided.

When shouts in the yard sounded at half-one, she hurried to the window, peeking through the heavy, velvet, lined curtains to see what had caused the hue and cry.

The household roused and Grace's heart tripped into full throttle. Had Dix been caught? A slamming door and the sound of running feet had her leaping to the wardrobe, where she stripped in record time. If Frau Shemper came to check on her, she couldn't be caught dressed to run. As neatly as she could, she rehung and refolded everything, shoving all that she'd packed back into the various places Frau Shemper had stowed them. She'd barely slipped into a gown and into bed, when there was a heavy tread and the scrape of the lock.

"Fräulein?"

It was the young guard, Wilhelm. She pushed up, bracing on her hand as if she'd been woken. "Yes?

What is it? What is the commotion?"

"An intruder, Fräulein. Nothing more. I'm to reassure you," he said in careful, simple German. "The man has been caught, so all is well."

Her heart sank. Dix, caught? In the hands of the Nazis?

"Who is he? What did he want?"

"The Führer's life, we presume," Wilhelm said sadly. "Some fear his greatness. Some do not understand how he has brought our country back from the ashes."

"I see." It was all the answer Grace could muster for the sickness in her gut. "Thank you. Is it safe to go back to sleep?"

"Of course, Fräulein," Wilhelm said, a note of pride ringing in his voice. "I will be on guard."

"*Danke*," she said, as he closed the door.

Grace cried herself to sleep. When she dreamed again of the SS officer, in his dark coat, dragging her through the snowy landscape, she wept again even as she dreamed.

Breakfast was a fresh interrogation. Had she dreamed? Had she seen the face of her fine, German husband-to-be?

To each question she offered a denial, a sorrowful negation of Hitler's quest to see her find her true love through the occult use of the jewel. With each day it got harder to lie. Was that part of the gem's magic?

Grace shuddered. She was back in her room, and she leaned on the wardrobe, staring into the long mirrored glass on its carved mahogany front.

The shadows beneath her eyes told of her sleeplessness. The dreams that sprang upon her the moment she closed her eyes, threatened to swamp her now, in her waking hours. They grew more detailed, more frightening.

Hard, vivid, sharp-lined images of the German officer dragging her into the night, shoving her into a car and driving hell bent for leather to a dark, dark building, then dragging her inside that. His ferocious, feral smile was all she could see before that door slammed behind them as well.

Every time, it was the slamming of that barn door, which woke her. Whatever awaited her in that barn would end her, subjugate her, and finish her utterly.

Her soul cried out against it.

And in between those terrible dreams and waking, she mourned for Dix. A man she hardly knew.

A perfunctory knock had her pasting on a false smile.

"Tea, Fräulein, before your afternoon walk with Herr Litzenfrund," Frau Shemper said, setting down the tray and pulling back the curtains to reveal a landscape of white.

"There will be snow for Christmas," she said, nodding. "A good luck sign."

"Yes, of course," Grace agreed, but her heart dropped. What day was it? It didn't matter, really.

She knew it was up to her to extricate herself. She was strong, strong enough to walk the many miles to the border, but she was no woodsman or gamekeeper, who knew how to befuddle her trail in the snow.

Snow would tell all too plainly where she'd gone.

Snow or not, though, she had to try. For the next two days, she talked endlessly with the generals, disappointing Hitler each morning with the news that none had sparked dreams. He was growing impatient, and waved the diary at her as they met in the Library.

"We will go to Berlin. I have been too long away. I must be there to make my Christmas speech. Germany has arisen from its death throes by science," he said passionately pounding the diary on the table to punctuate his words. "There is the mystical, yes, but it too responds to laws, does it not?"

He fixed her with a gimlet eye. "You are proof of this. I see you talking with my men, you are young, they are powerful, and yet none has captured you, or your jewel. It is as your diary says, it must be a specific one." He tossed the diary down, strode away. "They worry for my safety," he said, smiling now. "My generals."

The men around the room stilled, watching Hitler's every move.

"But," Hitler turned to her, pausing dramatically. "I am invincible."

"*Heil Hitler*!" *Gauleiter* Forster cried, saluting. Schmidt, followed suit and soon all the men were at attention, arms raised, saluting their leader.

"You see, Lady Corvedale? You will be aligning yourself with the best this world has to offer and your children will rule all of England when it falls before me."

That startling statement shifted something, and Hitler smiled. "And it will fall. Now, this is great excitement, yes? So." He moved back to the table, tapped the journal. "We will go to Berlin."

The change from rabble rouser, and madness, to practical German dictator was eerie. "Tomorrow. See to it, Schmidt. Tell Kempka to ready the cars."

"Yes, *Mien Führer*."

CHAPTER SEVEN

Frau Shemper was packing her bag. Her trunk from Calais, which the efficient housekeeper had taken away when she arrived, was open on the floor and more than half filled with clothes.

"I will be sorry to see you go, Fräulein," Shemper said, smiling as she carefully folded a woolen jacket. "But it is a great honor you are receiving, ja?"

"Of course," Grace managed to keep her tone light, her posture erect.

What she wanted to do was shove the old woman out the window, and run for it. Her grief for Dix weighed her down, though. She wasn't sure she'd have the strength to push.

Duty and honor kept her playing the game. She'd found no opening to secure the journal, or to get away, but by God, tonight she would make one. Dix had said there were tunnels, and servant's stairs. Too bad he'd only told her about them, rather than showing them to her.

No matter what, she must leave the house and

head for the border before daybreak. He had come and gone through the bathroom. Perhaps she could find her way that way.

She endured Frau Shemper's chatter, and took her evening meal in her room.

"It is an early start," Frau Shemper said, stopping to berate young Wilhelm for nearly tipping over the tea tray he'd brought up and set on the table between the fire and the settee. It was much smaller than the one Dix had lifted easily the first day she'd seen him.

That made her heart hurt more.

"I will wake you with plenty of time to dress and have something to eat, ja?"

"Yes, thank you, Frau Shemper."

"*Zer gut.* I will return for the tray and to warm your bed."

"*Danke.*"

The moment Frau Shemper left the room, Grace sprang into action. She wouldn't be able to take much, but she could make a pack of her clothes. She would wear the boots and kit she'd originally donned when she was to go with Dix.

A sob caught in her throat. He'd been willing to come get her out, free her, and had sacrificed his life to bring her a chance of safety. She couldn't stay here, meek and passive in the face of that sacrifice.

No time for tears," she admonished herself. Frau Shemper would be back soon so she had to hurry. With precision, she laid out the things she would take then repacked the trunk and bag so the items she needed were on top.

The books she'd been given from the library mocked her from where they lay on the floor. She shuddered to think of the horrible, horrible prose in both books, which glorified genocide.

"Cleansing" they called it.

"Murder," she muttered. Perhaps she, like Goebbels and his cronies, should indulge in a little book burning.

"Oh, no," she said, smiling as an idea occurred to her. "Not to burn," she added, picking both books up and stacking them together. "Burning's too good for you."

She ate heartily, worrying over the details of her idea. When Frau Shemper returned with a guard named Carl, she asked the woman if she'd stay for a moment.

"Ja, of course," Frau Shemper said, motioning for Carl to take the dinner tray.

"Frau Shemper, I'm a bit embarrassed, but I decided I would ask you." She made a face. "I have these volumes, which *Herr* Goebbels lent me." When Frau Shemper's visage took on an adoring look, Grace's heart leapt up. "Isn't he the most interesting man?" she sighed, her hand on Frau Shemper's arm. "I know he is married, but his smile is so..."

"Ja," Frau Shemper agreed, smiling as well. "It is."

"Oh, you do understand! Well, I read the books he recommended and I was hoping you'd let me slip down to the library and get the other two books..." Grace showed her the volumes. "Joseph...I mean Herr Goebbels recommended them so highly, and I thought...well..."

Frau Shemper colored prettily. "I see, ja, well, of course."

"Oh, thank you. I'll get dressed and..."

"No, no," Shemper waved that away. "No need. They have all gone to the trophy room to smoke and discuss things of importance to Germany's future." The woman smiled. "We will go together, ja? I will be your..." she seemed to be searching for an English word.

"Chaperone?"

Shemper beamed again. "Ja! Exactly. Come, come. We will go now."

The two women took the stairs at a brisk pace and arrived at the library. Luck was with her, as Carl came along the corridor at precisely that moment. Grace whispered to Shemper, "Might I have some fresh tea, Frau Shemper? I would like to read for a bit before bed."

"Ja, of course, but not too late?" Frau Shemper said, smiling. To Grace's delight the woman opened the library door and ushered her inside, turning back to instruct Carl to get tea for Grace.

Hurrying around to the wall where the books had come from, Grace re-shelved them, then picked out two more at random, along with a leather-bound volume she'd seen earlier in the day. Her diary lay on the table where she and Hitler had sat this morning.

She walked over, intending to switch the books, only to realize with dismay that the book on the table wasn't the diary. It looked like it, with its leather binding and deckle-edged pages, but she knew her diary.

She *knew* it and this wasn't it.

Damnation! She'd come for nothing, and if she was caught they'd be sure she'd switched the books. She had nothing to prove she hadn't.

Hurrying to the door, she was about to pull it open when someone grabbed her. She was unceremoniously jerked into the darkness. Before she could fight, a hand covered her mouth and a voice spoke low in her ear.

"Get back to your room. I'll meet you there."

Dix! It was him.

Dear Lord. He was alive.

"Nod if you understand."

She nodded vigorously and the minute he let her go, she settled her robe into place and walked calmly to the door without looking back. Her heart was dancing in her chest, but she kept her face serene. She pulled the door closed behind her just as Frau Shemper turned her way.

"Thank you Frau Shemper, I found the volumes I wanted." Frau Shemper examined the books and nodded. "Ja, these are very popular."

Carl, with a fresh tea tray, followed them up the stairs muttering all the way about soldiers being used as pack mules.

She made a point of thanking him politely. He waited for Frau Shemper as she saw to the bed with the warming tray another servant had brought up.

"In the morning then, Fräulein," Frau Shemper said, smiling and nodding to the books. "Don't read all night."

"Yes, thank you, Frau Shemper." It was all Grace could do not to shove her out the door.

"Go, go, go!"

Grace wanted to scream the words, but she held it in, standing by the table in her warm robe, cradling the books she was supposedly enamored of until the lock dropped into place.

The minute it turned, she dropped the books, flung off the robe and began to dress. She smoothed on fine silk stockings, not for fashion, but as an added layer of warmth under her thick socks. She pulled on her trousers and added a heavy woolen skirt over that. She tucked a shirt into the waist of the skirt and added a thick sweater over that, tucking it in as well. The heavy garments had the added benefit of disguising her slender shape somewhat.

There was a tap-tap-tap at the window and she raced to it, easing it open and helping Dix to climb inside. She shut the window and dragged the curtains closed behind him.

"Oh, Dix!" she cried, pulling him close, hugging him with all her might. "I thought you were dead."

After a split second hesitation, his arms closed around her with the strength of banded steel.

"Grace," he murmured.

"Who did they catch, then? Whom did they execute?

"Some poor bastard sent here to assassinate Hitler," he replied, holding her close, his chin resting on her thick hair. The silk of it under his cheek was something he'd never thought to want. Now that he'd felt it, however, he couldn't imagine not touching it, not running his fingers through it...

The thought was so poignant, so achingly pure, he had to pull away. He wanted so desperately not to feel the feelings, which poured through him.

They were dangerous, those feelings.

"I'm sorry," she said, letting go. He felt the cool air rush between them and suddenly ached for her. "I'm so sorry, it's just, I thought you were dead."

"No, it's okay," he soothed, curling a lock of hair behind her ear, stroking her cheek. He had to stop touching her. Had to. But didn't want to. "But we have to go."

"Yes, yes, of course." She scrubbed at her face. "I'm almost ready. You have the book?"

He nodded, stepping back from her, making sure he wasn't touching her, then handed her the book.

It disappeared immediately into the bodice of her shirt, and she quickly wrapped a long scarf around her midsection, securing and concealing the diary.

She already had boots on, but why a skirt?

Before he could speak, Grace knelt in front of the trunk, twisting the latches back one way, then the other. A soft click had him squatting down next to her to see what she had done. With one more twist, the front of the trunk fell open to display a smooth, slim compartment. There were Francs, Reichsmarks and a variety of other currency. She pulled out two passports, handed him one, and, hiking up her skirts, she loaded the remaining francs into the pockets of the pants she wore beneath.

"We can either be brother and sister or husband and wife."

"No way we could pass as siblings," he said softly.

She looked at him then, straight and steady. "You're right."

There was a heartbeat of tension between them, but his nod broke it.

"Here," she said, passing him a ring. "If it doesn't fit, I have a chain for it so you'll wear it around your neck. You're Rafe Leibenstrammer from Leipzig and I'm your wife, Greta."

She hefted the bag. "Let's go."

It took him a moment to realize what had happened. She had taken charge. She was ready to go.

Unaccountably, he felt light, happy. On top of the

world.

"Right. Come on." He held out his hand and she took it. He pulled her toward the door, listening carefully.

"Wait." She pulled free, and went to the bed, fluffing the blankets and moving the pillows so that there appeared to be someone in the bed. "Do we need the sheets for rope?"

Grinning, he shook his head. "We're going out the front door, so to speak. It'll take me a minute to pick the lock."

"Here, let me do it." She pulled long slim tools out of her boot and picked the lock with quick precision.

"To paraphrase your brother," he said, amazed. "You're bloody brilliant."

"He's not very good at locks." But she grinned at him.

Wilhelm, the young guard he had met in the woods, was on duty out in the hall. The more experienced guards were being used on the perimeter now, after the attempted assassination. A guard like Wilhelm was fine for interior duty, especially, they would think, on a woman who had given them no trouble.

"Put your head around the door, call him in."

She frowned at him. "Don't kill him if you can help it. He's only a boy."

"I know."

"Wilhelm!" She called to the young man. He jerked upright from where he had been leaning against the wall pretending not to sleep.

"Come quickly, there's someone outside the window. Come, quickly, there are ropes!"

He hurried into the room and never knew what hit him as Dix cold cocked him. The boy crumpled.

"Shut the door," Dix said, as he tied Wilhelm's hands. Together they dragged the boy behind the settee so he couldn't be seen from the door. They propped him there, pulling the heavy curtains to cover him. "We have to get to the lavatory."

"Lavatory?" she hesitated.

"The loo."

"Right." They slipped through the door, and Grace paused long enough to use her picks to relock the door. That would slow things down.

They slipped into the bathroom and he boosted her up into the attic, tossed up her bag, then followed, sliding the covering hatch back into place.

"Now what?" she whispered.

"I parked a truck on the old farm road. It's several miles walk."

"I was prepared to go the twenty to the border," she said with a shrug.

"You're a smart woman," he said, as they sat, letting their eyes adjust to the dark. "I'm going up to the roof to get the ropes. Not only do I not want them seen, we may need them."

"Hurry, then."

He was gone in the blink of an eye and she was left alone in the barren, dusty attic. She could see rings of light where various pipes came through the walls or ceilings of the centuries-old lodge, and into the echoing space.

In the deep silence, she heard voices.

Her heart picked up its pace until she could hardly think, but when nothing untoward happened, she realized what she was hearing. Hitler and his generals. They were still in the smoking room. Their voices carried easily into attic, carried along the pipes.

Moving slowly, Grace made her way across to where the voices were clearest. Braced on her hands and knees, straddling the rafters, she bent to listen.

The rapid pace of the German was hard to decipher at first, but she caught the rhythm of it.

"Ja, within the week."

"France will never stand against us."

"Our agents there assure me that we will have full access to the banks."

"So there will be the undermining first."

"Powerful men in high places."

"The spring offensive..."

The more she listened, the tighter she clenched her jaw. France would fall, at least the northernmost part. From what they were saying, the whole area was riddled from within by sympathizers, and played false by key business sectors who believed Hitler's results, his economic growth forms, were the way to go.

"Belgium," one said. "It should fall like a ripe peach as well."

Goebbels had left in the morning hours, so that had to be Schmidt or Forster.

"What of England?"

She froze in the act of moving back to her place by the bathroom hatch.

"We have an inside man, high in the government."

CHAPTER EIGHT

The name they bandied about meant nothing to her. Grace didn't know the man, but the Germans talked about the man's ambition. They cheerfully exulted over the possibility of turning England's streets into a blood-red ruin with all the men, women and children they planned to execute. And this man, this English traitor, would help them do it.

Her stomach sank as she heard names she did know, listed among the targets. Homesickness swamped her and she longed for London, burned to warn the men and women the generals were discussing as if they were chess pieces to be knocked aside.

Her heart faltered when she heard how closely they had come to assassinating King George VI, a mere two weeks earlier as he inspected troops in France. England had thought the king so well protected. And all the generals laughed at that. Grace's heart dropped. She had been one who'd told her superiors there would be no danger for him, as yet, in France.

Now she knew better.

She had a name.

As important as the diary and her notes on troops and timetables were, this information trumped it. She *must* get word, and the name, back to the Home Office.

There was a soft rustle away from where she crouched and she turned to see Dix materialize as if from shadows. Her heart leaped into her throat, this time with delight, as he easily navigated the thick rafters to reach her side.

He motioned her to rise and she did, wincing at her stiffened muscles. Something of her fear and panic must have shown in her face. He bent close.

"What is it?"

"When we're outside."

"Come, then," he whispered, taking her hand. His hands were so large and warm that, irrationally, the simple gesture made her feel safer.

They slipped through a narrow door and onto a landing.

"Servant's stairs," he breathed the words into her ear, making her shiver. "Step where I step."

It was a tense few minutes as she followed him down the tightly wound stairs. A few meters from the end, he stopped.

"At the bottom is a door. We'll slip out of it. This is the most exposed part of our journey. We must stay tight to the wall for two hundred yards. We'll reach a door. That opens on the back garden. Along the garden wall to the gate by the smokehouse. From there, we'll go out the back window and through the woods to the truck. Got it?"

"Hug the wall, door, garden wall, smokehouse, woods, truck," she parroted the instructions in brief.

"Good."

Her heart pounded as they slipped out, hugged the wall. They were about to cross the garden she felt a shiver of cold on her chest. She stopped, holding Dix at bay.

A struck match for a cigarette illuminated two of the soldiers with dogs stationed in the garden. They were nearly invisible amidst the shrubs. Their Alsatians sat or lay at ease, but their ears constantly scanned the night.

She caught Dix's sleeve, nearly embracing him to minimize the risk her voice would carry. "Dogs in the garden," she whispered.

That sharp jaw tightened and his lips thinned.

"What now?"

He hesitated, and there was a pinched, blanched look to his face. "Tunnels."

Tunnels? Why hadn't he said so? Why were they risking...

The answer snapped into her mind as clearly as one of the dreams. Dix's distress at being under the bed. His tension now at the mention of the tunnels. Small, tight places.

Many had a fear of them, and evidently this brave, almost recklessly skilled American was one of them.

Her heart clenched. They had no choice.

"I'm with you," she said, squeezing his hand. "We'll make it."

His only answer was a nod. He slipped past her to another door. It was locked, but he reached above the heavy doorframe and pulled down a heavy, but well oiled, key. The door opened soundlessly and he meticulously returned the key to its hiding place.

"Come."

They descended into the neatly kept, and obviously recently swept cellar. As they moved into the older, packed dirt section of the cellar, Dix stepped carefully from one hardened patch of dirt to another, leaving no trace of his passage. She followed suit. He seemed fine until they reached a stack of barrels in the back of the cellar.

"The tunnels start here," he said, pointing at a heavy cabinet next to the barrels. "There is a trapdoor."

"Do you have a hand torch?" she asked, keeping her voice brisk and practical.

"I do."

"Give it to me, I'll go first."

"No," he grated. "I'll do it."

She faced him in the dark, hands on his arms. She couldn't seem to stop touching him. And didn't care. If it was her destiny to marry a German, an SS officer at that, then she would take friendly contact, hopeless as it was, where she could get it.

"Dix, I don't know you well, but I know you are a brave man. I have my share of fears, but this isn't one of them. If there is light ahead of you, you can do this."

He closed his eyes and she saw the mental struggle as it passed over his face. Finally, without speaking, he handed her the torch.

Traversing the tunnels was a nightmare. She hadn't lied when she said that she had no fear of the dark, or the tunnels.

Spiders were a different story. She had a positive

horror of spiders.

It was winter though, she told herself, and they wouldn't be active. They would be sleeping. Maybe frozen.

Somehow that comfort got *her* through, and she, pulling Dix along behind her, got Dix through.

The tunnel terminus was a rocky cave. At the cave mouth, back from any view, Grace doused the torch.

"No," he said, then bit the word off. "Never mind."

She continued to hold his hand, pulling him to her side. This was a man who'd scaled the hunting lodge with ropes. A man who'd hidden plain sight, at risk of exposure at any moment, to rescue her as a favor to her brother and father. Not on orders, or because it was his assigned mission.

He'd done it for honor. For friendship.

Why couldn't she have dreamed of someone like him?

"Where to from here?"

"The truck," he rasped. "It should be two miles north of here."

"Okay. We should go."

"No, wait." He moved up next to her, and after a moment's hesitation, wrapped his long arms around her, holding her close. "Thank you."

She rested her cheek on his chest, listened to the steady beat of his heart. Nothing could be wrong in the world when someone like this could hold you so carefully, so protectively. So perfectly.

Held fast in his embrace, Grace let worry seep into the ground and dissipate. She felt renewed.

"You're welcome," she said finally, knowing they should go, but wanting this embrace to never end.

He stepped back. "I'm sorry, I shouldn't have--"

"No," she cut him off. "Don't apologize."

She picked her bag up before he could, shouldered it.

"Before we go, I need to tell you something. If we get separated, or if something happens to me, you have to get the diary and this message back to Standish."

She told him of the overheard conversation, gave him the name, and the key for deciphering the notes in the diary.

"If I'm killed, or recaptured, you mustn't try to get to me. Get to the coast, get to England. My father and the others must know that someone close to the King is a Nazi sympathizer. That, and the notes in the diary, are far more important than my life."

Looking up at him, she saw the argument in his eyes, in the set of his mouth. "No. It's the truth and you know it. We can't lose the monarch, not with everything else. George must continue to be seen as a strong, capable ruler."

"I'll come for you."

The words, so simply stated, cracked something in Grace's heart. She wanted to weep, to crow, to dance. But it wasn't to be. She was promised to another now, and from everything she'd read in the diary, that promise couldn't be undone. Whoever he was, he would find her and drag her into the snowy night. Then, Grace Corvedale would be gone.

"No," she said, going to the mouth of the tunnel. "My life for the King's life. It's a fair deal to save England."

Dix followed, and rested his hands on her shoulders. "I won't let anything happen to you,

Grace."

Tears sprang into her eyes, will you, nill you.

Shaking her head, she fought for control. "Don't say that."

"It's true," he said, and to forestall any other comment, he led her out of the tunnel and into the night.

It took them two hours to reach the truck. The snow, deep in some places, a mere dusting in others, hindered their progress, caked their clothes and chilled them to the bone.

The truck itself was dilapidated, rusted and looked as if it had been left on the goat track to rust into oblivion.

"Don't let appearances fool you," Dix said, his long strides carrying him to the truck more quickly. He pulled a key from his pocket and opened the door for her.

The civilized gesture in the middle of the woods fanned the flames of her appreciation for Dix. They stomped and brushed the snow off as quickly as possible, then started the truck. Grace didn't know cars, though she'd driven a good many of them. The heavy, satisfied purr of the engine when it turned over told her this was a well-kept auto despite its outer shell.

"I told you," Dix said, with that lightning smile. "Don't judge a book by its cover."

She held up her hands in mock-surrender. "I stand corrected."

With great care, Dix put the car in gear and they rolled over the crisp snow, following the downward path of the mountain.

"What's the plan, husband?" she said. "From now on, you must call me wife, or Greta, ja?" she added.

"Greta Liebenstraummer, my wife. No children."

"*Ja, zer gut.*"

"Do you speak much German?" he asked as they bounced down the rutted track.

"Enough, but when I do speak it, I still sound English," she said, watching him as he drove. His face was in shadow, but the bulk of him, his sheer size, was a reassuring presence in the drafty vehicle. The heater worked, but it was hard pressed to compete with the gaps in the doors and the cracks in the glass. "Where did you come up with that horrific accent you used as Franz?"

"Our gardener, at home, is German. He can speak English," he looked at her briefly, smiling, "American English. But he mutters to himself, and to my mother's roses, in German. I listened."

Astonished, she stared. "You learned to speak German by listening to the gardener?"

"I learned how to care for roses too."

"What other languages do you speak?"

"French," he said, grunting as he downshifted to take a rougher part of the road more slowly. "And Cherokee. Brakes on this are terrible. I tuned the engines, but didn't get to replace the brakes."

"You tuned..." she said, trailing off. "Well. How did you learn French?"

"My mother's French, from Verzey, not far from Reims."

"Champagne region. I've visited there often," she said, wincing as they hit a rut and she nearly flew into the air. The car tilted, sliding her over the seat to bump his shoulder. "Sorry."

"It's all right. Do you drive?"

"Yes, but I'm not sure I could manage this road."

"This isn't a road, it's a nightmare. We'll hit a farm road in a few minutes. We'll stop there and look at the map."

"Good. I have no idea where I am."

"The lodge is at Zweiburg. Hitler came in from the Saarland, according to his chauffer, Herr Kempka. They were taking you to Ludwigshafen today, to fly to Berlin."

"I figured I was twenty miles from the French border, where they took me across."

"Closer to thirty, but yes. Problem is we can't go that way. They'll be watching it. It's fortified along the old Siegfried Line on the German side, with new bunkers and constant construction. And you already know that on the French side, *Le Ligne Maginot* is full of bored soldiers waiting for Germans they can shoot."

"My contacts might be able to get us through."

"If we could get to them, yes. But I think your capture is a sure sign those might be compromised. It doesn't really matter. Our German friends expect us to go that way. So we won't."

"We can't go up through Poland," she said, working her way around the map in her mind.

"Nor can we go through Saarland, now that they've re-allied themselves with the Reich. But we'll head that direction."

He took the turns with competent skill, keeping the rattling old truck on the track, despite the rocks and stumps she saw looming up in the headlamps.

"We'll go up along the river to Kusel, then to Birkenfelt and on to Konz, south of Triers. My contact there will get us a plane. As soon as we can, we'll fly from there to the Netherlands to refuel, and then cross the channel. The Netherlands are still standing neutral," she heard the sneer in his voice for that.

"As is the United States."

"Yeah," he said, and his smile gleamed in the darkness. "So they say."

Flying. She hated flying. But if it got her out of Germany, she'd ride a rocket.

"The biggest problem is gas," she said, walking through the logistical steps.

"Yes. There won't be many petrol stations along that route," she said, as she tallied up the potential issues.

"You know it?" He sounded surprised.

"Not well," she admitted, "but the Nahe River valley produces Rieslings. I've been to vineyards in that area. They are fairly remote."

"I have extra fuel in the back, but," Dix let that hang for a moment as he navigated a tricky bit of ground. To her surprise, as the wheels caught again, the road smoothed out. "Not enough for the whole trip. And here is our farm road."

After a quick stop to relieve themselves and a check of the route Dix outlined, they moved on.

"You should get some sleep," Dix advised, "I'll need you to navigate later, but I know this part of the road."

She agreed, sure she wouldn't sleep, but within minutes, she had dropped off, and into the dreams. They were urgent now, more vivid than before. The menace she felt from the German was palpable. The fear. The sense of utter doom, which hung over her.

She jerked awake. Somehow, as she slept, she'd come to rest her head on Dix's leg, and she felt his hand slide out of her hair as she struggled to sit up.

"Whoa, whoa," he soothed. "Only a nightmare." He put a hand on hers where she had braced it on the rudimentary dashboard. "You're entitled to a few, after these last few weeks."

"Yes, I suppose." She sat in silence, then said, "You've been driving for hours. I can drive, if you need me to."

"I know. But we're not going much farther. By daybreak, we need to be under cover if we can. Neither of us are convincing enough as Germans, nor do we want to draw attention to ourselves in any way. They will be looking for us. Anything Hitler wants as badly as he wanted you, they will look for."

"I know."

"Tell me why. The diary?"

Grace considered it, but given what he'd risked, she couldn't deny his right to know everything. "Yes and no. I'm a servant of the Crown, as you know."

"A spy," he said, but his voice was teasing and light.

"If you like," she agreed, smiling as well. "That makes it sound far more glamorous than it is. I simply collect and pass on information I find in my visits to various wineries around France and Southern Germany.

"Hmmm. Yes, well, glamorous or not, if it keeps us out of a new Great War, then I'm deeply grateful."

"And that would be why I did it," she said, glad he understood. Her father had come back from France a changed man, according to her Grandmother Corvedale. And her uncles, the two she had never met, were buried somewhere near Somme. The land there at Somme, where the war was worst, had still not fully recovered from the blood spilled in such appalling quantity.

"If not for spying, then why were you taken?"

"I thought it was that, and when they took the diary I was sure of it," Grace said, curling her legs up onto the seat, but this time, she was careful not to encroach on his space. That had been far too lovely, far too comfortable a place for a condemned woman.

"And it wasn't?"

"No. Are you familiar with the article from the London Times about Hitler's rise to power? I believe it was reprinted in the New York Times as well."

"The New Orleans Times-Picayune carried it." He grimaced slightly. "The mystical is always news in New Orleans," he said, "And the article's references to Madame Blavatsky and the Thule Society's origins were added to the Times-Picayune article."

"Then you may understand this better than I thought," she said, relieved. "I didn't know you were from New Orleans."

"Yes, I live in Boston now and my business is there, but my family is in New Orleans."

"What do you do?"

"When I'm not being a soldier, you mean?"

"Yes," she said, smiling.

"I import tea, coffee and other spices, and sell them across the United States."

"Goodness, that sounds impressive."

She saw that flashing smile again. "Somewhat. But you were talking about the article. About Hitler and why he wanted you."

No better way than to blurt it out, get it over with.

"It's the brooch, the one I wear as a necklace."

"The gold and sapphire one."

"Yes. The diary tells the story of the necklace and its supposed magical power for the women of my family. It's hundreds of years old, dating before the 1100s and the conquest of Jerusalem, but it came to my family in 1314."

Dix frowned. "You say that like it was yesterday."

She laughed. "For the historians in my family, it was. My Aunt Grace, the one who takes to that kind of thing the most, seems to feel these long dead knights have merely stepped away for a quick smoke, or a cup of tea, rather than having been moldering in their tombs for centuries."

"That's a difference in our worlds, I guess," he said, softly. "Not that there aren't a vast number of those, but my family doesn't have that prestige."

"Really? Well, it isn't that important," she said, but she saw the look on his face. Evidently it was a sore point with him, so she quickly let it go. "What's important is that a legend goes with the jewel. It says the eldest daughter of the family is to receive the jewel when she comes of age. When she meets her destined husband, she will begin to dream of him, and must marry him, or terrible fates will fall upon her, and upon the family." She sighed. "The same is said to apply if one loses either the jewel or the diary, but that's been proven to be untrue."

"Really?"

"Well, the jewel was lost once, briefly, but recovered, so I guess we'll never know. And until now, no one was in a situation of peril that the diary and the jewel were endangered."

"How fascinating. Do you believe it?"

"I didn't, not really," she admitted. In the darkness of the car, with their lives in the balance, she was compelled to total honesty. And with him, with Dix, even more so. "And it hasn't been completely secret, you see. One of my great grandmothers loved to tell the story of how she and my great-grandfather fell in love. She was a flighty creature, unfortunately, and a terrible gossip. The story wasn't that interesting in face of new scandals, so it died away. But I was careless, I used the story to get information, to build rapport with a mother over the wedding of her daughter."

Grace looked out into the darkness. Nothing stirred, not even the wind, on the snowy landscape. The stars were hard, winking dots on a field of inky black. It was so cold, so very, very cold.

"Did you get the information you needed?" Dix asked softly.

"I did."

"Then it was what you needed to do."

She sighed. "Yes, it was, but that was the tipping of the domino, I'm afraid. Somehow the story got to Hitler. You know of his passion for eugenics?"

"You mean genocide?"

She shuddered. "Yes, might as well be that. He decided that my jewel might help him build his master race."

"Damnation," Dix said softly. "Beg pardon," he apologized, but his indrawn breath said he understood the gravity of the situation.

"No need. His historian read the diary, told him that he couldn't use it that way, according to the book. Only I could wield it. And until I passed it on to my daughter, should I have one, it would lie dormant."

Dix saw the flaw in the plan immediately. "And if you died without passing it on?"

"I don't know." She shifted restlessly on the seat. "It hasn't happened, not in all the centuries. Even when it was lost, even the one time where a mother passed the gem to her daughter at a very young age, it's stayed in the family."

"Where did this thing come from?"

"We have no idea. Some think it's from Egypt," she said. "The lotus flowers, the etchings in the gold are all ancient Egyptian symbols, but that could mean nothing. The Egyptian Empire was, like the British Empire, vast."

"Yes." Dix stopped at a crossroads, checking the map. He turned north, and took up the thread of the conversation. "So it shows you your true love?"

"No."

Her answer was so curt and short, Dix turned to look at her.

"It doesn't," she answered defensively. "It shows you who you're destined to marry."

"Ah," he said. "So not all these marriages have been happy ones?"

"I didn't say that. I said the book doesn't talk about love. It talks about destiny."

"These people didn't love each other?"

"Of course they did, but that wasn't the guarantee. Only that the gem would show you, in dreams, your destined mate."

Something in her voice alerted him. "You've had dreams."

She felt the panic and tears well up, sitting like a huge stone on her chest.

"Grace?"

"Yes," she said, finally. "I dreamed."

"And?"

"He's a Nazi."

CHAPTER NINE

The silence deepened in the car. Dix didn't know what to say. He believed in magic, or at least in those things you can't always explain. While his parents attended a protestant church every Sunday, they certainly believed in the more mystic side of things, and so did he.

How could he not, growing up in New Orleans with a passionately French mother, to whom everything was a sign, and his father's Cherokee heritage as well?

Dawn was breaking when he saw what he needed.

"There, that's what we need," he said, pointing off a ways into a fallow field. "A barn. We can pull the truck around behind it, out of sight."

"Won't the farmer wonder, or forbid it?"

"No, not these days. Times have been hard, and as long as we don't leave a mess, or set it on fire, farmers here won't begrudge us rest in their barn."

"All right."

Dix put the truck in reverse and backed down the

road to the edge of the field. He eased the truck into the field at the tree line, so his tracks wouldn't be as visible as they would running straight to the barn. The road had been clear, and didn't betray their passage, but the obvious tracks of the truck in the field were something he'd have to see to.

The labor of that, and the time would give him room to think.

"Grace, I don't know if there's a solution to what's going on," he began, "but if there is, I'll do my best to help you find it."

He looked steadily at her, once he turned off the truck's engine. "Where there's a will, there's a way," he added.

She nodded, not meeting his gaze. "Thank you. I don't know what it would be. But I can hope."

"Good. Now, take your bag and I'll get the blankets from the back of the truck. We won't be able to have a fire, but I have some bread and cheese, a bottle of wine, some sausage, enough for a cold meal."

Together, they heaved open the large barn door, slipping into the sweetly hay-scented, and very full, barn. The crop had been bountiful and the bales were stacked to the rafters of the modest building. This farmer's cows would not go wanting, no matter how bitter the winter.

"We'll stack the bales like this," he said, pulling some down to form a square. "That way, we can block the drafts from the doors."

"This building is so well built, there's not much of one, even with the door open," Grace noted, pulling down a bale.

"You're strong, for a woman," Dix complimented.

"Thank you. I often have to move boxes of wine. I guess that's why."

When they had the bales stacked it was noticeably warmer in the tight square of space.

"Get comfortable," he said. "I'm going to go see if I can hide our tire tracks. Brushing them out will leave a trail as well, but up by the road at least, perhaps it won't be noted. Right now, anyone hunting us would easily find us.

"I'll help."

"No, you rest. It won't take long," he said. Not only did he want to spare her the labor, but he needed the space to think.

Grace watched him button his heavy coat back up and go out into the breaking day. He carried a hatchet and a look of determination.

She shut the door, and the first thing that popped into her head in the silence was about Dix.

He hadn't laughed at her.

As she spread the blankets over the hay, she realized it was important. He hadn't laughed. He hadn't denied or fobbed off the idea of a destiny, or the magic the jewel possessed.

And he'd gotten the diary for her.

Pulling her knees up to her chest, Grace rocked in place. The world was going to hell in a handcart, and she was destined to marry a Nazi, a proponent of an ideology she utterly despised. Her time with Hitler's generals, and with the man himself, had added to her revulsion. Their passionate belief that people born with differences--a little slow, a hand or foot that hadn't fully formed—-were somehow unworthy to live? How could that be?

And the sheer hypocrisy of it appalled. Joseph

Goebbels, one of Hitler's supreme *Gauleiters*, was himself, in fact, deformed. Yet he was the master of twisting the words, and making the unthinkable not only plausible, but probable.

She shuddered as she remembered Goebbels eyes on her. His hands holding hers around the books had been clammy, his fingernails untrimmed.

At least he was not the one. He was too short.

"Stop thinking about it," she remonstrated with herself. Needing to do something, anything constructive, she laid out the provisions from the large knapsack Dix had brought in from the truck. She arranged the cheese, dried figs, dry sausage and bread on a large napkin and found a metal cup for the wine.

Dix returned from his labors fairly quickly. "I brushed out the obvious tracks, but there is traffic on this road. I didn't want to be seen."

"Good idea," she said, patting the blanket. "Come and sit. It isn't *Le Navire* in Paris," she added, "but it will do."

"*Le Navire*, is that a favorite?"

"Yes, the chef there does amazing things with seafood."

"Hence its name."

"Yes, The Ship." She smiled at him. "The restaurant itself is said to have been constructed from broken parts of a ship wrecked in a battle on the Seine."

"Intriguing," Dix said, with a laugh. He picked up the metal cup, into which she'd poured wine, and lifted it in a toast. "May we someday get to sit and enjoy a meal in *Le Navire*, in more peaceful times."

He passed her the cup, and she lifted it to her lips.

"Amen," she breathed into the cup, sipping and swallowing around the lump in her throat, and passed it back.

They made quick work of the meal, sharing the lone cup back and forth until they'd finished most of the bottle. The wine helped fight the chill, as did having food in her belly.

"We need to get some sleep. I'd suggest keeping watch, but I know that I can't, and you probably can't either. We've been up too long."

"I think we would hear anyone driving up," she said, unfolding the extra blankets so they could wrap themselves in them and snuggle into the hay.

"But if they find us, there's nowhere to run."

"Then we'll hope for the best."

"Indeed."

To her surprise, Grace was able to drop off to sleep right away. And the dreams didn't torment her, at least not right away. She and Dix slept back to back, and the heat of his body warmed her through.

When she did wake, it was because of Dix.

"No, no," he muttered, beginning to thrash, still asleep. "Don't shut it." He spoke more, but it was in a quick, accented language she didn't recognize. The words had a musical lilt, but it was obvious from his distress that this was more nightmare than dreams.

"Dix," she dodged his flailing arm and shook him, hard. "Dix! Wake up!"

Her brain couldn't process the speed with which he moved.

One moment she was shaking his shoulder, the next she was pinned underneath him, a knife at her throat. The wild fear in his gaze was that of the dreamer.

Fear threatened to paralyze her, but she managed to speak, slowly, carefully. "Dix," she said. "It's me. It's Grace."

When the wildness in his gaze didn't ebb, and he didn't speak, she slid her hands up, palms open. Infusing a sharper note into her voice, she took a different tack. "Lt. Robert Dixon. Soldier," she snapped. "Report!"

Sense came back to his eyes, and the tightly clenched jaw relaxed. Confusion came next.

"Grace?"

"Dix." Relief nearly undid her control. "You had a nightmare." She kept her voice steady, and her hands open. "You reacted when I shook you awake."

He looked down, seeing the knife. Color flooded into his face.

"Oh, my God." He rolled off of her and to his feet in one fluid motion. He stood like a bewildered bull, staring at the knife in his hand. "What did I do?"

"Nothing. You didn't do anything." She rose, carefully. "You didn't hurt me."

"I could have,' he said bleakly, staring at the knife. He sheathed it at last, turning his back to her. His breath was long and uneven. "I could have."

"Dix?" she said, softly. "Come here."

"No. I need to sleep in the truck. I can't risk hurting you."

Grace shook her head but he didn't see it, of course. "No, it's too cold. It's warm in here, inside our hay fort," she said smiling, finally, as her heart rate returned to normal. "You have nothing to apologize for, and I won't hear of you going to the truck. Now, come back to bed."

He pivoted then, eyeing her. "I told you I'd sleep in the truck."

"And I told you to come to bed," she said, hands on her hips. "And I mean it."

"So do I."

The argument was so ridiculous, his face so thunderous, that she felt a laugh bubble its way into her throat.

"No," she said, fighting the grin. "It's warm here. It's cold there."

"I'll sleep outside."

She couldn't help it, she laughed. "You'll turn into an icicle."

His face was thunderous with temper, but somehow, she wasn't afraid. This was anger, yes, but embarrassment too. And it wasn't that blank, unreasoning stranger looking out of Dix's eyes. It was Dix.

"Why are you laughing?" he demanded.

"Because I can, I guess," she said, still grinning. "I'm free. I'm warm. And I just ordered a man to my bed," she giggled. "Oh, my God, I think that's a first."

Sitting down, she let the giggles come at the look on his face, his reluctant smile. Despite his embarrassment, he'd gotten the double meaning.

He made a sort of growling noise, but she could hear the laughter trying to find its way out.

"Oh, to your bed is it, Lady Grace? You English can't order us Colonials around anymore you know." His mock-anger was countered by the laughter in his eyes.

"Ah, but we can." Standing, she put on her most haughty air. "Mr. Dixon, I have given you a distinct request," she said, pretending to peer through a *pince nez*. She pantomimed sweeping aside a voluminous train and sat, her back sternly erect. "As the hostess of this fine establishment, I order you to return to bed."

"Mademoiselle," he said, bowing with courtly grace, playacting on his own merit. "I thank you for your invitation, but..." he lifted his hands in a truly Gallic gesture of surrender. "I fear I am no fit company for a young lady of your quality."

Her heart stuttered. When had they gone from playacting to reality? He had meant that. He didn't feel worthy of her. That had been the utter and most sincere truth.

"I beg to differ," she said softly, making her decision. "Most sincerely."

She unbuttoned her coat, and laid it aside. Her boots were by the knapsack, as were his. She removed the scarf next, folding it neatly on her coat before unbuttoning and pulling off the heavy skirt.

He watched her like one of the big African cats watched a gazelle, but he didn't move.

"I'm a woman, Dix. And my fate is uncertain."

"War's coming," he grated. "All of our fates are uncertain."

She nodded, glad he'd admitted that. It would make this easier.

"If my fate *is* sealed by this jewel I wear," she said, unbuttoning the topmost shirt, then the one underneath so she could pull out the diary and set it on top of her skirt. "Then I want to share myself now with someone I like, someone I trust." She smiled now, unbuttoning the first button of her trousers. "Someone I find attractive."

"Grace," he growled, striding to her, stilling her hands on the buttons. "You don't have to do this."

"I know," she said, looking up into his dark, dark eyes. "That's the point, Dix. I don't have to. I get to choose. In this at least," she said fiercely, "I get to choose."

"Grace," he said softly, lifting a hand to cup her cheek, then bringing the other hand up, to tangle in her hair. "We'll get you away. I promise you."

"Yes, I know," she said, standing on tiptoe to brush her lips over his. "But we could lose this time. We very nearly lost the last one. Germany could win. The man I've seen could be responsible for the life or death of my family. I would marry Satan himself to save my family, so would you."

He nodded, then slid both hands into her hair. Pulling her mouth to his, she nearly drowned in his deep, powerful kiss. It rocked her, heart, mind and body. Every nerve seemed to be afire, every sense heightened as he drew her closer.

She would have pulled him to the straw, taken him without another word or thought, but he stopped, panting. He moved back, made a little bit of room between them.

"Grace," he began.

"Shhh," she said. Whatever he had to say, she'd probably thought of it and discarded it. Except one thing. That might be what was worrying him. "I'm not inexperienced, Dix. Not totally. I was engaged."

He tipped her chin up so that they were looking at one another in the clear, but dim light coming into the barn. "And?"

"We were friends at university, and briefly, lovers. But he wasn't for me. He recognized it before I did and we broke it off. I wanted it to be him," she said softly, with remembered sadness. "But my Aunt Grace was right, there were no dreams, no omens or signs. Just a good man who realized that I didn't love him."

She leaned in, setting her cheek to his chest, listening to the steady beat of his heart.

"I want you, Dix, for who you are right here, right now." She tilted her head, met his gaze with all the courage she could muster. "And yes, I know that I'm using you. And I hope you'll forgive me."

She looked away and fought back the tears. She didn't want this to be about sorrow. She wanted it to be about triumph.

"If I'm to be shackled to destiny's choice, then now, here, I choose to experience joy, unbridled and unfettered by whatever power lies over me because of the jewel. Give me this, Dix. Please."

He watched her, giving her time to compose herself, but not so much that her nerves got the better of her.

"My Lady Corvedale," he said softly, "your wish is my command."

Unbearably relieved, she closed her eyes, squeezed them shut until she was sure she wouldn't cry.

"Why thank you, Mr. Dixon. It is to be my pleasure, I assure you," she added impishly, trying to lighten the mood.

"I will contrive for it to be so," he said, sliding his hands inside her shirt to caress the satiny skin of her back. He watched her carefully, keen for any sign that he was pleasing her. He understood what she wanted. She was certain.

If this was to be her memory of freedom, he

would make it as wonderful as possible, given the circumstances.

"I'm sure you're up to the task," she murmured as his lips met hers. Slowly, nibbling little kisses over her lips and cheek, he peeled away her shirt. She stood, in trousers and her brassiere, like a conquering goddess in a field of golden hay. Her fingers quickly worked the buttons of his shirt, but she wasn't quite tall enough to push it off his shoulders.

Lips locked to hers, he tugged it away. She pulled his undershirt from his pants, to run her hands up his back. She smoothed the long scar there, and pulled him closer.

"Touch me, Dix," she implored, and his mind, which had locked in place as she explored, began to work again.

He unhooked her brassiere and let it slide to the hay. He left her enticing mouth long enough to taste the curve of her neck, then knelt in front of her so that he could lavish attention on the beautiful breasts he'd exposed. Their tightly budded points were enticing and he drew one into his mouth, warming it and teasing it with his tongue.

She moaned, fisting her hands in his hair. "Dix," she whispered. "Dix."

"Yes, Grace, I'm right here. Tell me how to touch you, how to pleasure you."

"Kiss me again," she said, tipping his face up to hers as she bent to kiss him where he knelt. Her strong hands kneaded his shoulders, bared now under her searching fingers.

She slid down to kneel as well, dragging her pebbled nipples over his chest, enticing him with her mouth and tongue as she moved along his body.

Her glorious hair was loose and he used it to pull her close again, feast on her mouth, lavish her with kisses.

Her hands were busy at his waist and when she loosened his trousers and freed him to her touch, he nearly died on the spot. Her soft hands shivered up and down the shaft of his erection, and he quivered in her grip.

"Grace," he growled, striving to hold on to the shredding bonds of his control. She bent her head and licked at his nipple, nipping it gently. He nearly came in her hands.

"Grace," he said again, pulling her hands away, trapping them in one of his, behind her back. "Two can play at that game of tender torture," he murmured, suckling her until she moaned.

He released her hands so that he could caress her backside, the sweet, soft globes of her bottom called to his hands and he used that grip to pull her to him, pressing himself to her center.

That too, nearly made him lose control for she was wet, and hot.

"Dix," she whispered, her hands tight on his hips, holding him in place. "Oh, that feels so good. You aren't inside me and already, I feel so good," she moaned, tugging at him, pulling him down to the hay. "Come inside me, make me feel..."

"What, Grace?" he murmured. "What do you want to feel?"

"Alive," she said, her gaze boring into his. "Safe. Whole."

"Cherished," he said, softly, laying her down, and shifting to lie beside her, his hands gliding down her body, over her legs, and up between them.

"Needed," he said, as she opened for him, tried to pull him over her and into her.

"Not yet, Grace," he said with a smile. "Let me do this."

"Dix," she said, "I need..."

"Yes, you do," he said, sliding a hand between her soft thighs. There, as her father had said, was the crown, the birthmark. He bent to kiss it. "You are my queen, with your crown."

He slid a long finger gently into the curves of her body, the wet folds parted and she rose to meet him as he dipped two fingers into the heat of her, the tight, firm power of her response nearly sent him as well. She cried out as a powerful orgasm overcame her. She rode his hand, bucking into his palm, giving him everything she had.

"Dix," she gasped, her hands pulling urgently at him. "Dix, I need you, I need..."

"Shh," he soothed. "I'm here."

"Dix," she implored, and relief flooded her face as he rose over her, slid into her with a groan of near-painful pleasure.

"Ohhhhhh," she exhaled the word, rising to meet his thrust. "Ohhh, yes."

"Grace." Her name flowed out with his breath. She was around him, and in him, their breath streamed together as he bent to kiss her. Deeply and powerfully they kissed, but her restless hips drove them apart as she arched back, driving herself onto him with a groan.

"Dix, Dix," she cried out, fighting the second orgasm.

He lifted her hips and slid forward, and she gasped in pleasure.

"Now, my love," he said, "together."

With long sure strokes, they built the pleasure to its peak. Her hands were like a vise on his hips, pulling him back in, harder, tighter, each time they moved.

"Look at me, Grace," he said, barely able to think, barely able to hold on to his control. "Look at me."

"Dix," she breathed. "Ahhhh, Diiiiix."

"Yes," he cried out as his body could take no more of the intensity of the pleasure they'd wrought together. She pulled him close and he exploded like a thousand suns.

Light, heat, a blinding sense of rightness, of fitness and perfection, rolled through him as he released everything to her. Nothing he'd ever felt before compared to that incredible blast of release.

Together they roared to completion. Quaking in the aftermath, hearts pounding, bodies slicked with sweat, they collapsed into the blankets, panting.

A bird called outside the barn. There was a faint rustle as the wind teased the few cracks in the walls. Time continued to move, but Dix didn't care.

"Dear God in heaven." Grace was the first to speak. Her voice was breathy, and faint, and he immediately shifted so he lay at her side. "Don't go," she murmured.

"No, I'm not going anywhere," he said, pulling a lock of hair out of her eyes so he could smile down into her face. "I was crushing you though."

"No," she denied. "You weren't."

"Hmmm," he temporized. "This is better though. I can look at you, enjoy you."

She blushed, but made no attempt to cover herself, and evidenced no regret for what they'd done.

She was beautiful. There was no other word for it, he decided, as he let his hand slip down her side, shaping her hip, and ghosting along her outer thigh. Gloriously beautiful.

"What?" she said, a touch of worry in her gaze.

"You." He smiled. "Your skin is like silk."

"Thank you." She returned his caress, flattening her hand against his stomach. "You're strong. So much muscle. Here." Her fingers danced over his chest to his shoulders, giving him a shiver of delight. "And here," she said, drawing his leg over her body to caress the length of his thigh. "So very strong."

"Grace," he said, leaning down to kiss her again, and to touch her face, her neck, her beautiful taut breast.

Her hand slid back to his hip, pulled him to her. "You want me again," she murmured, and her tone was full of wonder and delight. "Already."

"Yes." He wasn't ashamed to admit it. His body, spent and exhausted only moments before, was rousing at the memory of the pleasure they'd shared. "But we need sleep."

"Touch me again, like you did before," she whispered, ignoring his comment about sleep, and pulling his hand from her breast, down her body to the juncture of her thighs. "I want you to touch me," she said, meeting his gaze. "Please."

It was the please that did it. He could no more resist her than a drug anyway, but her wanting him, wanting what they could do together, was more than he could stand against.

"With pleasure," he whispered back, gliding back into her wetness, her center. "Are you sore at all?"

She shook her head, and pressed into his hand.

"Inside me, slip your fingers inside me," she demanded. And when he complied, she moaned out a long, heartfelt, "ohhhhhh."

"You like that."

"I do," she agreed, her gaze blurry with passion.

He slid down their bed of hay, pressing kisses to her belly and hip as he continued to slip his fingers in and out in a slow steady rhythm.

"Do you like this?" he asked, bending to put his mouth on her, stroking the shaft of her womanhood with his tongue.

Lightly, side to side, he let his tongue caress her. He could feel the tension building in her, closing her body around his fingers until she arched up once again, crying out in the intensity of her release.

"Ahhhhhhhh!" her cry was long and loud in the deep silence of the barn and it made him feel like he had conquered the world. Her pleasure, her utter release, was like the strongest of spirits, like a pure jolt of wicked, powerful electricity.

He let her settle, hardly daring to move as the aftershocks quaked through her. His erection was so stiff, so painfully full, he wanted to plunge in, allow the release that hammered like thunder in his brain, but although she wasn't a virgin--and thank the Good Lord for that--he didn't want to hurt her. Lovemaking like they'd done it, twice, might be too much for an inexperienced woman. He could hold back, even if it killed him.

He slowly let his hand slide away, pressing kisses to her thigh, and the curve of her hip as he moved to lie beside her once more. He leaned on his hand, elbow on the ground and stroked his other hand down her body, as her breathing returned to normal.

When she opened her eyes, he smiled. "Better?"

"Oh, my God." It was all she said, and he had to laugh.

"Is that good?"

"Better than good."

"Then you can get some sleep, finally." He cursed inwardly, but he would be a gentleman, he would restrain himself. "We've still a long way to go."

"Do we need to leave before dark?" she asked, rolling to her hip, matching his posture of leaning on one arm, letting the other hand rest on his side.

It was killing him.

He wanted her to touch him so badly.

"No, not before dark, which should give you at least two more hours of sleep."

"Are you tired?"

"Me?" he said, startled. He was so focused on her, and on mastering his body, that the question surprised him. "No."

"Good. We'll sleep when we're dead," she said, and pushed his hip so that he rolled onto his back.

To his delight, she straddled him, and his cock grew more rigid with need. Brushing her breasts over him, she rose up, pressing her lips to his, teasing him with her body.

"I don't know much about all this," she said, echoing his earlier thought, "but I love to learn."

She let her hips drop so that her body grazed his rampant erection, calling to it, dampening it and making him nearly drool with need.

"Teach me," she whispered. "This time, tell me what pleases you."

"You please me," he said, hands at her hips to pull her in.

She resisted.

"Too easy. Be more specific. I live for information."

"My beautiful spy," he managed, but his brain shut down entirely when she pressed the heat of her body onto him, sliding her wetness up and down the length of his steel-hard shaft.

"This seems like a thing to do," she murmured, sliding down again, "And that you like it, since your eyes crossed." He heard amusement and a joy in her feminine power infusing her voice, and smiled.

"Oh, I do like it, very much," he rasped.

"Tell me," she said, her voice husky and low. It sent shivers of primal need through him.

"What I want," he said, his own voice harsh, "is to bury my cock inside you, to hold you close, to kiss you until you can't breathe, and can't think. Until you can only feel."

"Ummmmm," she murmured, still gliding slowly up and down, her body now swaying slightly from side to side, heightening the sensation. "What else?"

"I want to come up behind you," he said. "Next time," he said, his hands cupping her backside. "I want to come up behind you and hold you to me. I want to tease your breasts, and kiss your neck until you nearly come just from that. Then I want to slide into you, fill you."

"Ahhhh," she rose slightly, teasing the tip of his cock with her core. "Like this?"

She dropped down, sheathing him fully so that he gasped at the onslaught of pleasure.

She started to rise, but he held her in place, grasping at the tatters of his control. Her questions, her body, her glorious, magnificent body, were driving him mad.

"Like that," he finally managed. "But from behind, so that I can touch you, caress you as I slide in and out of you."

"Ohhhh," she said, arching up from where she'd rested on her hands to lean back, her body bowed as she struggled to ride him. "Ohhhh, that sounds so delicious. Ohhhh, I need to--"

He could take no more.

With as much care as he could muster, he reversed their positions, letting the momentum drive him deep into her body so that they both groaned.

He wanted to plunge and buck and spend himself instantly within her, but he held on, barely, wanting to draw out the pleasure for her.

"Oh, now, now, now," she demanded, her hips frantically shifting upward as she sought to draw him in more deeply.

"Now," he agreed, thrusting forward as she rose, and they both exploded into orgasm once more.

This time, it was a long time before he could think coherently enough to move, and still, as he did, she wrapped her arms around him.

"I'll crush you."

"S'all right," she slurred, exhaustion finally sneaking up to claim her. He suspected she hadn't had much rest the whole time she'd been in captivity.

He slid next to her, pulling the blankets over them both. "Rest," he said.

"Yes. You too," she murmured, eyes closed. She snugged herself next to him, and within seconds her steady breathing told him she slept.

"Yes," he agreed, his own heavy eyes closing.

CHAPTER TEN

The slanting beams of the setting sun woke them both.

"*Bon nuit*," she said, opening her eyes.

"*Et tu, aussi*," he murmured, kissing her.

They stared at one another for a few moments.

"Regrets?" she asked.

"I thought I got to ask that question?" he teased, kissing her again. "None. You?"

She closed her eyes and smiled, her body moving in a curving, sensuous fashion that had him stirring with need for her again.

"None. Ever. No matter what happens, I have this."

He lowered his head to rest his brow on hers, her silky hair teasing his cheek. A feeling rose in him, deep and powerful. What he had felt, back in her room at the lodge, with danger all around them, was a pale shadow to this fresh wave of emotion.

"Yes. We both have this precious time."

"Dix?" He heard her anxiety, and answered it.

"It's nothing to worry about," he reassured her, glad that the fading light hid his eyes. "Though I'm concerned about time, and distance. We need to get you home. The further away from Germany you are, the better."

"Yes." She was looking at him quizzically, but when he smiled again, she let it go.

"I want to make love with you again," he murmured, "but it's later than I thought. We have to make Konz tonight to meet my contact."

"Then, as much as I want you too, we should pack and go," she agreed. With an economy of motion, but the grace of a goddess, she rose from the nest of rough blankets and rustling hay.

He wanted her with a desire that was fierce and hot, but he banked it down, hard, and hurried to gather the blankets and gear as she dressed. He dressed as well and together, hand in hand, they slipped from the barn, making sure the door was tightly closed behind them.

The sun had disappeared by the time they bumped back through the field and onto the road. The sky was still streaked with gold, red and grey, but the colors faded quickly into the dark of a December night. They made good time skirting the border, taking country roads as the moon rose. They held hands as they drove.

The silence between them was comfortable. Restful.

She'd never felt restful with a man. Usually, the men she'd met, or dated, or interacted with in business reacted to her in one of three ways. They were intimidated, they tried to intimidate her, or they were nervous as cats.

This easy camaraderie was novel, and welcome.

"We're approaching a little town," Dix said, slowing. "There's a checkpoint."

"I can fit behind the seat," she said. She'd been looking behind it searching for the source of the constant draft. There was a piece of the floorboard missing behind the seat, and that was what let in the frigid December air.

"Do it," he ordered, pulling a beret and a cigarette case from his coat pocket. He jammed the hat onto his head, lit a Gauloises cigarette and puffed it a few times. "I will be French, yes," he said.

"*Mais oui*," she joked as she managed to slip between the back of the seat and the hard, cold metal of the truck's frame. "It's quite disgusting back here," she commented, eyeing the trash, as well as the encrusted dirt that layered over the back of the seat and clogged the springs.

The truck slowed and she heard voices outside the car. She managed to roll most of the way under the seat, despite the dirt, pulling her coat up to cover her hair.

"Quiet as a mouse now," Dix whispered.

"Heh, another roadblock? What is this?" he said in a kind of guttural French she had heard in the streets of Paris. The man was talented, it was amazing. She also recognized his strategy, going on the offensive the moment he rolled down the truck's cracked window. "Why are you protecting Luxembourg?" he called to the guards, adding a braying laugh to the comment as he worked the character he was portraying.

"Papers," the road guard demanded as he walked

up to the door. There was a rustle and she smelled the strong French tobacco wafting into the night.

"Cold out there," Dix commented, puffing on the cigarette. "This is ridiculous. No one is invading Germany." He laughed at his own joke and she heard the guard chuckle as well.

"Here," the man said, and she guessed that Dix's papers were being handed back. "What's your business?"

"Business," Dix replied, braying another laugh. "Picking up supplies in Triers. Wine. Contraband whiskey from America. More cigarettes." The strong, distinct Gauloises smoke streamed out the window and she heard the guard's appreciative noise.

"Do you come back through here?" the guard had stepped closer to the car.

"I do," Dix answered. "You have something you need, my friend?"

"You really get whiskey?"

"I do. And unless you're asking in an official capacity, about the whiskey, then yes, I can. If you're asking as a German soldier, then I'll answer differently than I would for a friend." Dix paused, and she could imagine him flashing that wicked white smile. "What's your name, friend?"

"Oscar Kirshelm. How much? For the whiskey, friend?"

"For you, it's cheap. Twenty Reichsmarks."

"Twenty?" the guard spluttered.

"Twenty," Dix reiterated. "Its forbidden fruit, friend Oscar. What do you say? Do I bring you a bottle or not?

There was a pause, and one of the other guards called to Oscar and he shouted back, but she couldn't understand the words.

"Get me two bottles," the guard said, quietly. "I'll pay you when you deliver."

"I totally understand, friend. Here, have a Gauloises on me." There was a flurry of activity at the window, and she heard more calling, but this time, the guard said they were clear.

"I'll be back through before morning, friend," Dix lied. He let out the clutch and eased the old truck forward until the gears caught, then they were moving through town. He rolled up the window, but murmured to her, "Stay out of sight a few moments yet."

She heard the calls of the guards, and the call of a newspaper boy, selling late papers, telling of German forces sinking a British ship in the North Atlantic.

"What day is it?" she asked, when he told her she could come out from under the seat.

"It's the twenty-third of December."

"More than a month then, since I left Paris." She shrugged out of her coat, now gummed with dirt from under the seat. She folded it and set it on top of her bag, which rested on the floor.

"I'm going to pull off the road," he said, suddenly.

"Why?"

"I see trucks behind us, big ones. They may be troops. And they may be hunting us."

"Or?"

"They may be moving to fortify another part of the border."

He scanned the road ahead, looking for a turn off. There had been a road on the map, it led north on a parallel route to Triers before cutting east.

"There," he said, slowing only enough to make the

turn. He gunned the engine and sent them up the tree-lined road. As the road curved, making it invisible from the main road on which they'd been, he swung wide, turning them around to face the direction from which they'd come. He rolled the car to the graveled edge of the pavement and cut the engine and the lights.

"Let's see what we're dealing with."

They waited in tense silence for the trucks to catch up, and pass their hiding spot. Dix rolled the window down to listen. Before long they heard the grinding of the truck's gears as the transports climbed the rise in the road.

"They're loaded heavy," Dix said, listening.

"Troops," she said. "Let's hope they're going to Saarland or to the fortifications the Germans are building along the border, and not to Konz."

"Exactly," he said, taking her hand once more. He wanted the contact, the warmth of her touch.

The trucks rolled into view. Three of them. And behind them rolled a sleek Mercedes sedan with flags flying from the front quarter panels in pennant fashion.

"SS," Grace hissed, noting the swastikas, the insignia on the doors. "See, there on the bonnet, there's a badge. This is someone important."

"Not Hitler. Not enough cars."

"No. This car wasn't at the lodge. I would have recognized those. I watched them come in, made note of the bonnet signatures, and the flags."

"Encoded in the diary?" he asked, his tone light.

"No," she said with a smile. "That's reserved for the very important. For the cars, I wrote it down on a piece of paper."

Dix laughed and they let the quiet of the winter night soothe them as they gave the trucks and mysterious car time to get well ahead of them.

"Dix, when we get to town, I have to try and make contact."

He didn't answer her, merely turned in the seat to face her, raising her hand to his lips.

"I know. I think we'll have to split up, however briefly." He considered it for a moment. "There is an inn in Konz, small and catering to farmers and locals visiting family. We'll go there. We'll rest there for a bit, then make our separate contacts."

"We'll need safe words," she said, remembering her training. "Passwords."

"Yes," he agreed, thinking for a moment. "When I return, I'll say something like *Avilii, open the door*, and I'll use that word, specifically. If you hear that, it's safe."

"What does it mean? Is it Latin?"

"No, Cherokee," he said, glancing at her. "It means wife."

That stopped her for a moment. Did he mean...no. They were masquerading as man and wife. The thin gold bands on both their hands proved it, didn't it? A sham, nothing more.

"And if it's unsafe?"

"I'll say something about Char, as in, *I think that is my friend Char,* and you do the same. Avilii if it's safe, Char if it isn't. I'll have to wait for daylight to get to my contact. That means we'll be exposed."

"Yes. And if I'm caught, or someone recognizes me and comes for me, I need you to do something."

"What?"

"I want you to take the book."

Shocked, he shook his head. "You've come this far--" he began.

"I know. We've been lucky. I have the jewel, but without the book, Hitler can't find out any more of its secrets. I don't think they had time to copy the book." She smiled, adding, "It's long, and very detailed. And the varying scrawls of my lady ancestors are sometimes very hard to decipher."

"Have you read it all the way through?"

"Yes. Until now, I thought it a lot of fanciful stories. I thought it was a legend, which built on itself, because the women in my family wanted it to be true."

"Until you dreamed," he said, bringing out the thing that was most fearful. "And knew them for real dreams."

Watching him closely, she nodded again. "You aren't laughing at this. You believe it."

It was his turn to nod, and he squeezed her hand. "My grandfather is Cherokee. He has...let's just call it a certain *power*. If Grandfather tells you something came to him in a dream, it's time to listen up."

"I see." She pondered that for a moment. "Is America beautiful?" she asked wistfully.

"I've not seen all of it," he said, smiling. "But what I've seen is beautiful."

"Maybe someday..." she started, but let the words trail away.

"Yes." It was all he said. They both knew what lay ahead.

They were walking into fire when they reached Konz. If they were lucky, they would be warmed and on their way. If they were unlucky, they would burn.

A new Great War was upon them, if the signs were

to be believed. The years since the last war had seen wonderful advances in technology, in manufacturing. And all of that would make this war worse than the first.

"I'll introduce you to New Orleans," he said, and that quick grin lit the darkness. "And my mother. You'll like her, and she'll like you."

She laughed, but as she was appalled at how much she wanted to see New Orleans, meet his mother, and see the vast country that was the United States.

"I doubt that," she said. "Mothers never like the women their sons bring home."

"True, in most cases. But she would like you."

"I'll hold you to that," she said, but the words, like the thought, broke the mood and returned them to the night, the cold, and what lay before them.

"Here," she said, as she untied the sash and pulled out the leather bound journal. The soft, supple ties, which kept it closed, were frayed with age. "Keep it safe. Get it to Standish or Shippingston."

He nodded, doing as she had, tucking the journal inside his shirt. Her blouse and sash had hidden it more effectively. After a moment, he shifted the book to lie along his spine, then secured it with his belt and shirt.

"Do you think they've gotten far enough ahead?" She said it, looking forward, not meeting his eyes. She felt naked without the journal. Bereft. But it had to get home and Dix was the best way to make that happen. Now she only had one duty left.

"I need you to promise me something," she said. He gave her a sharp look as he buttoned his coat, shifting to settle the book into place.

"And?"

"If it comes to getting the information about the Nazi in the Home Office to my father and Shippingston, or saving me, or the book, you'll choose to get the name to the Home Office. The Nazi sympathizer was supposed to kill him when he visited France this month."

"King George was in France? What the devil..."

"Troops, or so the Germans indicated. I knew they were building them up along the front. Ever since September, and the declaration of war, they have moved troops into place, but nothing has come of it. I never expected His Royal Highness to come to the front lines, to speak to and inspect our troops there."

"And they were supposed to kill him?"

"Yes. But the generals said the informer chose not to, that he believed he could get more information by keeping George alive."

"You'll tell them yourself," Dix stated, starting the engine and letting it warm for a few moments before he turned on the headlamps and put it into gear. He looked at her briefly. "When you get home, you'll tell them yourself."

They rolled down to the crossroads and Dix turned to follow the path of the trucks. Grace felt destiny closing in on her the moment they made the turn. A sense of doom filled her, and she felt cold all over.

"Of course I will," she said, spitting in the face of that feeling. She would do whatever it took to survive, and to keep her beloved country safe from Germany. Even marry a Nazi if she had to, then use him, and everyone around him, to save England.

"Grace," Dix began.

"No. I understand." She drew in a deep breath, tried to stop the cracking of her heart as they drew closer and closer to Konz and the final leg of their journey together. "You are trying to cheer me, keep me focused on positives. You are right."

When he didn't answer, she sighed. "How much longer to Konz?"

"An hour, maybe a little less."

"Then I'm going to rest as much as I can."

He paused, but nodded in the dark. She could barely see it, or him, but she felt the movement as much as saw it.

"That's a good idea," he agreed, patting his thigh. "Rest your head here, and sleep."

Grace squeezed her eyes to forestall tears. She wanted him to be cold, or businesslike. She wanted him to be an operative. Instead, he was being kind. What she imagined a lover--a real one--would be like. It was breaking her.

Without speaking, she pulled her sticky coat up over her legs and lay down, head pillowed on his muscular thigh.

"There now," he said, stroking a hand down her thick hair as if he were memorizing the feel of it. "Close your eyes."

"How did Char get you to buy a horse?" she asked, when she could be sure her voice was steady.

The question, out of the blue, made him laugh.

"Your brother is very persuasive," Dix said.

"He is. He can sell more cases of wine, brandy and spirits than any three of us put together," she said, pride ringing in her voice. Char was a consummate deal maker.

"I can believe it," Dix said. "We were going to see

possible troop placements," he began. He kept his voice soft, his words deliberate and slow as he lulled her with his voice. "Char decided we should take a detour to a horse show."

She chuckled, and he continued. As funny as the story was, and typical Char behavior, she found her eyes drooping and her breathing slowing as his voice soothed her.

She was asleep.

He'd deliberately tried to comfort her with the story, keeping the funnier parts to himself. He would tell her the tale in true, full fashion another time, when she could appreciate the laugh.

As brilliant as she was at keeping that vaunted English reserve and mastering her emotions, he could see the cracks. The situations, mystic and real, were taking their toll on her.

The only medicine he could offer, right now, was sleep.

They'd stayed up most of the day yesterday, making love. He smiled into the darkness as he stroked her beautiful hair. Some of the long strands lay loose on his thigh, having escaped from the pins she'd used to secure them. He let it slide, thick and smooth, through his fingers.

Remembering their time in the barn, his body tightened. She was magnificent. Beautiful. Brilliant. She was everything he'd ever wanted, but didn't know he needed.

And she belonged to someone else.

The hour passed too quickly. In the depth of the night, with the clouds piling up, it seemed like they would never reach Konz.

As they reached the outskirts of the town, it began to snow.

"Just a room," Dix growled at the innkeeper. "We have business in town." He kept it simple, straightforward. Grace had easily slipped into the persona of a "proper" German Frau, waiting by the doors, the suitcase at her feet, her head down, her hair properly pinned under a kerchief, her coat still tightly buttoned despite the warmth of the Inn's front room.

"Of course, of course," the matronly innkeeper handed him a key. With miserly precision, he counted out the Reichsmarks needed to pay for two nights.

"There," he snapped. "Two nights, though it is a high price you charge."

The woman looked affronted, but quickly blanked her expression. The rooms were more highly priced than other places, and the bathroom was shared, but it was quiet.

"Come on, wife," he ordered Grace, and she looked up, her eyes startled. "I got you quiet, though at a dear price," he said roughly, but let his voice soften. "You and the babe will have some sleep, eh?" He took the bag from her, and tucked her hand in the crook of his arm as they headed for the stairs.

He heard the innkeeper sigh. Without telling her directly, he'd now led her to believe that his wife was pregnant. He'd also implied that though he thought the rooms too expensive, he paid so his wife would have quiet.

Perfect.

They reached the room, and shut the door.

"Oh," Grace said stretching and shedding the dirty

coat. "Look at that bed."

The bed was a marvel of carving and fanciful woodwork. The linens were simple, the blankets at the foot were plain, and obviously for warmth rather than décor, but the bed? It was a fantasy of art.

"It's beautiful," he agreed. Walking to it he ran a finger over the whorls of foamy waves surrounding an equally beautiful carving of a mermaid.

"When do you meet your...friend, husband?" she said, hearing the faintest noise outside the door. "I hope your business goes well."

"It will," he dropped his voice into the growling tone he'd used with the innkeeper. "Or I'll have payment for this winter journey from him before I leave. Never you fear, wife."

"Yes, Rafe," she said meekly, looking at him with a twinkle in her eye. "Whatever you say."

They both strained to hear if their watcher was still there.

"You should lie down."

"Yes, I am tired," Grace said, playing along with the charade. However, she also began to strip. Slowly. Peeling off the layers and setting them aside.

"Here, I will help you," he growled, aroused now, though they both stayed in character.

"You should lie down as well," she said, softly, trying to remember how to say things in a more common form of German. There were dialects, and slang, and the perfect diction and vocabulary of the schoolroom would give her away more quickly than anything she might say.

Dix said something that she couldn't translate, and when she did, the idiom escaped her. His pantomime, however let her in on the joke and she grinned.

"*Ja, bitte*," she said eagerly, pulling off her blouse and heading for the bed.

He joined her there, rolling her underneath him and smiling down into her face. The feel of him was like a match to dry tinder. She wanted him so much. With a will of their own, her hips arched into him, feeling him already hard and ready for her.

"Do you think our watcher has heard enough?" he whispered in her ear.

It was like a bucket of cold water. It was all show.

Of course. For the listener.

Turning her head to the side, she could no longer see the shadow of feet at the door. She nodded. "They're gone."

"Good," Dix growled, and claimed her mouth in a kiss that left her breathless.

With frantic hands, they tugged at each other's remaining clothes. She bit his shoulder, then kissed and stroked the spot to soothe it, only to drop her head back and moan softly as he slid a hand between her thighs.

"You," she insisted, writhing against the coverlet as he drove her up. "I want you. Inside me."

With the strength of need, she flipped him, pinning him in turn. She kissed his belly, making the muscles there quiver, as she undid his trousers and yanked at them to pull them down.

"Yes," she cried, taking him into her mouth, and nearly sending him into orgasm with that one simple stroke. Fisting his hands in the blankets, he held on, tortured with pleasure as she laved the tip of his erection, let her mouth heat and wet him until he was nearly mad for her.

"Enough," he demanded, pulling her up, taking her mouth in a powerful kiss. "I want to be inside you when I explode, not fly off the handle like a green youngster. But your mouth," he said, claiming it again for a long, deep kiss. "Your mouth is a wonderful thing."

She smiled and tossed her brassiere, her last remaining item of clothing, to the floor.

"So is yours," she said, coming back for more kisses. "It's like a drug for me." She kissed the corners of his mouth, drew his bottom lip in and gently closed her teeth on it, erotically tickling it with her tongue at the same time.

"Lift up a little," he ordered, and she raised her hips. Guiding her down, he impaled her on his cock, watching her eyes fog with passion.

"Ohhhhh," she let her hands rise up, instinctively, to caress her own breasts, bringing the tips to pebbled points, making him insane with need.

He shifted his hips and she groaned again. He rose up to claim a gorgeous nipple, cupping the other breast in his hand as he did. Her hands slid into his hair and held him close as she rocked her hips into his, driving him deeper into her body.

"Come here," he demanded, rolling them sideways, easily shifting her underneath him. He could feel, and see, that she was about to come, about to explode at any minute, and her rocking, rocking, rocking on his cock was sending him there as well. But this was no barn in the middle of nowhere.

To solve the problem, he captured her mouth in a searing kiss as he thrust forward. Her moan was lost in the power of their tangled tongues.

"Now," she insisted, her eyes flying open to meet

his gaze.

"But quietly," he said, barely hanging on. "We can't..."

He lost the thought as she undulated her hips and brought him in.

Everything focused on her, on that moment, on them.

They rose together, as if by design. Her lifting hips, his thrusting cock sent them both over the brink. Light exploded behind his eyes, and he managed to keep the ecstasy he felt to a long, guttural growl, rather than the shout of triumph that was trying to explode from his chest.

Grace, in turn, was biting her lip, eyes closed, head thrown back. The muscles in her neck were a distinct line as she, too, held in the need to express the power of the moment.

He rocked into her, drawing a gasp as the aftershock caught her and the thrust titillated her as well.

"Mmmmm." She managed to keep the sound soft, but he heard the pent up power of it.

"You like that?" he whispered, lowering to her as he gently rocked inside her. Her body was still quivering from their mutual orgasm, pulsing in the aftermath, as was his. But he could do more for her, bring her to completion again.

Slick with their passion, he felt the clenching and unclenching of her inner muscles, and he timed his short, rocking thrusts to that feeling. She was so tight, her every response was like a ripple on his cock.

Her restless shifting told him he was bringing her to a fresh orgasm and he braced on one hand and rose a little higher so he could flick a light finger over the bud of her pleasure. The thickened folds, the blood-engorged feel of it, told him she was right there. Ready.

He timed both thrust and light strokes until he felt her rise up hard to meet his hips. This time it was her hands clenching the blankets as she rode over and through the powerful, vibrant release.

She was magnificent.

The thought rang in his mind, over and over. Grace. His Grace. Magnificent.

Gently and carefully, he eased out, despite her protests. "I'll get you a towel," he said, remembering to use German.

There was a washbasin and water, and sturdy towels. He dampened one and brought it to the bed.

"Here," he offered it, meeting her sleepy, relaxed gaze and feeling the grin split his face at her satisfied demeanor.

"*Danke*," she murmured, watching him. Impossibly, he felt himself stir again, as she slid the towel sensuously down her thigh.

"Get dressed, woman," he mock-growled, forcing himself to turn away from the luscious sight. He turned back, smiling. "Or we'll never get out of bed," he added, as softly as he could and still be heard.

She'd stopped when his voice turned harsh, but smiled now, and stretched like a satisfied cat in a patch of sunshine.

He wanted her. Desperately.

Now.

That same unfamiliar feeling swamped him and he stood, nearly dumbstruck, as he realized it was love.

CHAPTER ELEVEN

Grace walked briskly along the street to the market, her kerchief tucked firmly over her hair. She'd brushed the dirt and grime from her coat and wore her heavy skirt. She carried a market bag, having left the traveling bag in the room. The papers she'd had concealed in it were now tucked into her waistband, where the journal had rested.

She felt it's absence. It was like an ache, knowing the diary wasn't in her possession. But it was the right thing, giving it to Dix.

Her thoughts circled like frantic birds when she thought of Dix. He was a good man. Strong. Brave. Intelligent.

Forbidden.

She stumbled as the word sprang to mind, but it was true. The sidewalks had been swept clear of snow, but there were icy patches, so her clumsiness nearly sent her sprawling.

She was so focused on her footing, and the sudden burst of cold in her chest, that she didn't see him.

"Fräulein Corvedale," a man said from her left, his voice cold, hard, and sure. "We meet at last."

The black coated man, SS insignia in bold red on his fine woolen coat, silver badges gleaming, stepped into her path, gripping her arms. His hard jawline and the cruel set to his lips mad her gasp in shock.

"No. It can't be." She struggled in vain to free herself.

"Ah, properly cowed, are you?" He laughed as she shrank back, tried again to pull away. Her struggles only amused him. "My reputation precedes me, I see. You should be afraid Fräulein. You are a clever woman, but what the Führer wants, he keeps."

Soldiers closed in around her and the SS officer pivoted, her arm still painfully held in a crushing grip, and marched her forward. One of the guards trotted forward to the corner, waving his arm. By the time they caught up with him, the black Mercedes, which had passed them in the night pulled to the curb.

"Fräulein," the officer said, when the door was opened. "You can go in willingly, or I will put you in." He squeezed her arm painfully, and leaned in to whisper in her ear. "And I might enjoy that a bit too much."

Grace tugged her arm free, and he let her go. She was under no illusions as to his strength, or determination. His blue-eyed gaze was hard, cold. It was the first time she'd seen his eyes. In the dreams, the eyes were always shaded by his hat, his head tilted down.

Frowning at the image in her mind, she slid into the luxurious car.

Something was different. Something was wrong. She closed her eyes and let the threats and self-aggrandizing boasting wash over her. What was it? What was different?

The blow took her by surprise and she fell forward, striking her head on a case sitting on the floor of the car. Vaguely as her head spun and her ears rang, she heard him ranting about her lack of attention, her insolence.

"The scars," she murmured, her mind finally latching onto the difference in the image. "There were scars."

A second blow, driving her into the case once more, sent her into darkness.

A man burst into the cellar where Dix was meeting with his contact, Frans Bruener. They were shaking hands, concluding their business as the man hurried forward, spewing information as he came.

"The lady, they've taken her. SS," he panted. "Put her in a car."

"Grace," Dix snarled, gripping the man's shoulder. "Where did they take her?"

"Not sure. Not far though. He struck her. The SS man."

Fury roiled through him, rage so powerful, so red, it must have shown on his features because the runner shrank from him, fear written on his face.

"Describe the man," he said, through gritted teeth.

"SS, black coat, you know." The man swept a hand down his body to indicate the length. "Long. Boots, of course. Close cut blond hair. Blue eyes."

"Do you know him?"

"Major Rudolph Kirken."

"Find him."

The man looked at Bruener, who nodded.

"Done," the runner said, going out as fast as he had come in.

"You will take care of him." Bruener made it a statement, not a question.

"Thoroughly."

"The plane will be ready. If you come for it, it will be there. If you don't..." Bruener shrugged.

"You'll have an extra plane. I'd use it if I were you, if we don't make it. Get out of Germany."

Bruener nodded. "I have my own way." He turned back to the table where they'd been sitting, picking up the packet of documents and an envelope of money. "Your people made sure you would have plenty."

Dix peeled off half the money, handing it back. "If we're not out of here tonight, we're not going. We'll be dead. You take this. Get yourself and your family out." He took a scrap of paper and scribbled an address. "If you need help, or when you get out, send word to this address. They'll find me. I'll do whatever I can."

Bruener held out a hand, and Dix gripped it. "Thank you. My wife, she's from a Jewish family. We had already planned to go."

"It's only going to get worse."

"Ja," Bruener agreed. He stepped away, opened a drawer in the desk he'd been using. "Here. Take this."

The luger wasn't new, but it was well cared for. The action slid easily as he checked the load in the clip. It had been reworked, but he didn't care as long as it fired.

"Thank you."

He was heading for the door when the runner

burst back in.

"The lady, they called Herr Doctor Nurin to come. I heard them tell him to come to the station on the Triers road.

"Take me there."

"Good luck!" Bruener called after them. He looked at the notes in his hand, folded them and tucked them away. He hoped he didn't have to sell the plane.

It was cold, and the wind whipped through Dix's hair as he crouched by the building, listening for the sound of footsteps. The guards, four of them, were switching off rounds. Two walking, two inside with Grace, the doctor and the SS officer.

The first of the two called an insult to his comrade over his shoulder as he turned the corner. Dix was on him before he could make any further sound, dropping him quietly into the snow when he stopped struggling. He slung the man's rifle over his own shoulder, and shoved the extra knife into the side of his own boot. As quietly as he could, he stuffed the man's body under the edge of the house and stood up.

The second guard strode around the corner and stopped, a supremely surprised look on his face as the bayonet on Dix's stolen rifle slid into his heart.

Dragging him and dropping him with his fellow, Dix crouched at the corner near the building's front. The other two guards would be coming out soon. He had to be ready.

"Hey!" A voice shouted, only for the sound to be whipped away by the wind. Dix spun in place, and in one smooth move, threw the knife from his boot. It caught the guard in the throat and he went down, gurgling, his hands frantically scrabbling at the hilt.

A click behind him had him turning, but the second shot wasn't a misfire. It caught him in the back, spinning him around, dropping him to the ground.

The soldier advanced, pointing his weapon down at Dix, murder in his eyes. "We have her," he said. "And now, you will die."

Grace vomited so hard she thought her head would fly apart, though nothing was coming up. The doctor made soothing noises, and gave her a cloth to wipe her mouth, which she somehow managed despite the manacles on her hands. The doctor had a cold compress for the massive bruise on the side of her face, and, now that her sickness was over for the moment, he returned it to her cheek. She groaned in relief.

"It is the blow to the head," the doctor said quietly. "It has upset your inner ear." He helped her to sit on the desk again. He had cleared it of papers and laid out a sheet where he put his bag. Opening the satchel, he uncorked a bottle.

"Take these, now," he said, passing her two more tablets. He'd tried this once already, but she'd vomited up the first set. "They will reduce the swelling from inside, as the ice will help outside. We will see if you can keep them down now, eh?" She gave him a miserable look, but nodded, and he patted her hand. "It will pass, Fräulein. I am sorry for your trouble. Now hold this on your cheek, ja? I want to check your--"

Whatever he was about to say was cut off as the

two soldiers in the other room hurried into the night, letting a gust of freezing wind blast into the small building before the heavy wooden door slammed shut. It was a station or local political office during the day, but Major Kirken had commandeered it when she threw up all over his highly polished boots.

She'd still been vomiting when the doctor arrived and ordered Kirken into the other room so he could examine Grace.

Kirken had demanded his suitcases, and when one of his men brought them in, he'd changed his clothes right down to a new pair of boots. The soiled boots he tossed carelessly into a trash bin, along with his trousers. She could see the pile of cloth and leather from where she sat, since Kirken wouldn't let the doctor close the door.

Now, she saw Kirken draw his a pistol, and go to the door.

He opened it and the temperature dropped again.

"Heidle, Paulkirk?" He shouted into the wind.

Grace heard the faint reply, but couldn't make out the words.

There was a triumphant "HA!" from Kirken, and he rushed into the night, the wind slamming the door behind him once more.

"Herr Doctor," Grace began earnestly, but the doctor stopped her.

"I cannot help you Fräulein. My position in town is already in jeopardy. Everyone knows I was called here, that Kirken had you. If you suddenly escape, who will he blame? And who will help my wife, my children, my patients if I am dead?"

Grace nodded. He was right. And even if he would help, she was in no shape to run.

"Now, see if you can stand, ja?" The doctor helped her, his grip firm, but gentle, in high contrast to Kirken's heavy treatment. "Good, yes. Now, sit again. Dizzy? No? Good. I will give you something for the pain."

There was a muffled sound outside, and she and the doctor glanced at one another. When it wasn't repeated, the doctor shrugged and checked her eyes.

"I do not think there is a concussion. Here, take this," he said, offering a spoonful of a sticky liquid. "It is not much, but it will make you sleep. If he knows you are asleep, drugged, he will not hit you again, ja?"

She had lifted it to her lips, taken a little, when the door whipped back, slamming into the wall with the force of the wind, and the furious Major Kirken. His uniform was askew, snow-caked and blood stained. While his hat was firmly in place, incongruously, the belt on his coat dangled loose.

His jaw was set, but already swelling as if he'd taken a blow. His lips were a thin, hard, cruel line, but his eyes were shaded by the cap pulled low over his face. A purpling bruise rose high on his cheek, at the edge of his left eye. He'd taken a beating from someone.

Her heart, already bruised and battered, sank to her boots.

If Kirken were still here...

"Come," he said harshly, grabbing her arm and jerking her off the table, pistol at the ready. He left the doctor standing alone, a spoon of medicine poised in midair.

Kirken dragged her behind him, letting go for a fraction of a second as he snatched her coat from the hook and flung it at her. Before she could put it on, he yanked her forward to the door.

"You," he snarled back at the doctor, "go to town, report that my men are dead."

"But..."

The weapon came up, and the doctor stopped speaking.

"This woman is my prisoner, wanted by the Führer himself. Nothing," he snapped, "*Nothing* will keep me from getting her to him. Do you understand me?"

"Ja, of course, Major Kirken," the doctor stammered.

Kirken dragged her out into the night. Her head swam and her vision clouded. The blows, sickness, and the little bit of the drug she'd taken were working to skew her thoughts and have her hallucinating.

The scars.

There were scars on his face. She saw them, on his cheek, plain now as he turned away from the lights of the station, dragging her to the car.

Had she missed them before? Had she been so afraid of him that she missed them?

It really was Kirken, then, who was her destiny. This abominably cruel, furious Nazi was the one. He would deliver her like a present to his master without a qualm. This was what the jewel, cold as ice against her breast, had brought her to.

The bruising and his high, turned up collar hid his face as he shoved her into the car. He didn't bother to shake off the snow, which covered him everywhere. He shoved her across the front seat and slid in behind her, still pointing the gun her way.

The engine roared to life and he spun the wheel,

sending Grace flying into the door. He reached over and jerked her upright, driving into the night with reckless skill, returning to Konz and taking the turn in the middle of town that led toward Triers.

There were few people on the streets as dark was falling, but they stopped to stare at the racing car, fear on their faces when they saw the flags, the insignia.

"And you do nothing," she whispered to them. Her head swam and her thoughts spun like a strand of spider silk on the breeze.

She tried to focus, tried to form words, but the medicine and the sickness blanked her thoughts and she slumped, exhausted and spent, to the seat.

When she came to, the manacles were gone, but he was lifting her, pulling her from the car. The barn from her dreams was awash in the Mercedes's powerful headlamps.

Her sudden struggles made him lose his grip, and his shouts where whipped away by the wind. She resisted, trying with all her might to pull away, to get away, but he was too strong.

Inexorably, he pulled her to the building, jerked open the door, and all but tossed her in.

"Grace," he said, his voice hugely loud as he shut the door, and shut out the wind.

She stepped back, away from him. "No."

He threw the hat aside, flung off the coat. "Grace, it's me. It's Dix."

Motionless, she stared at him. "No, I'm hallucinating. I'm dead."

To her joy, he laughed, then winced. "No, you're not dead. And I thank God you're not badly hurt."

"Are you?" she said, seeing blood, bright and red

on his shirt. "Are you?" she rushed forward, pulling his arm over her shoulder, guiding him to sit on dusty bench. There was a dim light from a string of bulbs high in the top of the barn, but her focus was on Dix.

"Where are you hit?"

"In the back."

She came behind him, around the bench and pulled the black shirt from the waist of the black pants. He'd changed into Kirken's clothes, right down to the belt.

"What happened to Kirken?"

"He got frostbite," Dix said, then hissed as she slid the diary from the waistband of his pants. Blood dotted the leather, and a long scratch made a sort of divot along its surface.

Beyond the scrape, a tear in his skin seeped blood. He'd been shot.

A second hole, two inches beyond the entry point, showed where the bullet had gone out.

"Oh, Dix," she breathed his name like a prayer. "You've been shot."

"Dammit," he cursed, craning his neck to see. "No wonder it hurts like hellfire. Is it bad?"

"No," she said, and the relief made her faint. "No, it's not bad. A bandage should stop the bleeding."

"There's probably a first aid kit here, somewhere," he said, looking around.

Tearing her eyes from the still seeping wound, Grace looked up. And up.

It wasn't a barn, it was a hanger. In front of them rested a biplane, painted a shiny, bright blue. Beyond that, a work bench and a small office promised the possibility of a first aid kit.

Hurrying over, she found it and came back to

bandage his wounds.

"The book saved you," she said, finally, holding it up for him to see the bullet-scored binding.

"It redirected the bullet."

"Yes."

"Grace," he said, taking her hands. "Kirken's dead. He's gone."

She said nothing, and he plowed on, fear stalking his heart.

"It was him, wasn't it? The SS Officer from your dreams."

She shook her head. "No, it wasn't"

Despair churned his gut. "We'll fly out of here at first light," he promised. "You'll be safe."

"I'm already safe, Dix," she began. She had to explain it to him, help him see.

"No, Grace, I'll protect you. Marry me," he said, dropping to one knee. He winced at the pain in his back, but repeated the words. "Marry me. If you're already married to me, you can't be forced to marry him."

Joy blossomed within her. "I won't have to marry him, Dix. *You're* him." The words tumbled out, and pulled him to the bench, gripping his hands. "In the dream, all I saw was his jaw, hard and sharp," she said, stroking a hand lightly over Dix's bruised jaw. "And scars, here," she pressed a gentle kiss to the three parallel grooves that lay on his cheek under and above his left eye. "And the hard twist of the lips," she said, kissing him.

She bent her head to kiss his hands, his raw knuckles.

"And the uniform. That hated uniform."

"But..." he began, but she saw the realization dawn

in his eyes. "It's me. I wore the uniform. I dragged you out into the darkness."

"To save me."

"Yes," he said, that lightning smile she loved crackling into full blown laughter. "Yes!"

"So, I'm safe, you don't have to sacrifice--" she began, but he cut her off.

"Hush," he said, pressing a finger to her lips. "I love you Grace Corvedale. If you'll have me, I would be the happiest man on earth if you would do me the honor of becoming my wife."

Heart full, she returned his smile. "When you put it that way, how can I say no?"

"I'd rather you said yes," he said, caressing her cheek, tucking a loosened strand of hair behind her ear. "Will you?"

"Yes."

He whooped, pulling her to him in a crushing grip, then winced over the pain in his wound.

"Ow," he complained, but he didn't let her go.

At noon, when the wind died down, they rolled open the doors of the hangar to a freezing but clear day. A soft breeze twitched a tattered windsock where it hung from a rusting pole. It twitched only a little, the way a cat's tail twitches when it's relaxed and happy.

They had spent the better part of the night checking the plane, pulling out anything that would slow it down, stripping it as much as they could to conserve fuel.

"Now it's my turn, I guess," Grace said as they loaded in what few supplies they'd scrounged from Kirken's car. They'd found a full hamper of food in the back, so they had at least eaten well before they finally slept.

Kirken's car was in the hangar. The case on which Grace had hit her head was full of documents pertaining to troops and fortifications along the border with Luxembourg. That was the only luggage they loaded into the plane.

Grace changed Dix's bandages again, and dusted on sulfa powder to prevent infection. With that, they were ready to leave. If the wind favored them, they'd be in England by suppertime.

If it didn't...

Dix checked her harness and kissed her one more time before he climbed into the second seat and strapped in. The air was cold and grew colder as they rose. The small towns and cities over which they flew on their circuitous route seemed remote and toy-like in the clear air.

Grace didn't take a full breath until she recognized the topography of Belgium. She'd had been sure, by compass headings, that they'd flown over Luxembourg, but there were few distinguishing features between Germany and Luxembourg on the route she flew.

They were making for an airfield at the RAF base in Kent, at Eastchurch. She could only pray they wouldn't be shot down on approach.

The plane had no radio, and little in the way of comfort. It had been a show plane, and a crop duster, and never meant for passengers. If Dix's message had gotten through, if any of the pigeons he'd told her about had gotten through, the RAF would be watching for them.

They might not make it to Eastchurch. They

might run out of fuel first. She and Dix had discussed it, but both had deemed it worth the risk.

With a tail wind though, they could make it.

The sun was setting, and Grace shivered more with fear than cold. She hated flying, and in the dark it was a nightmare. The old plane's instrument panel was unlit and they were over the channel.

Hard, gusty winds had hit them broadside as they crossed from the mainland to the sea. It had blown them south, but she had idea how far.

Grace checked the compass again. If the heading was correct, they wouldn't miss England, but she wasn't sure now that they would actually make it *to* the coast.

Suddenly she saw it. A light silvered on in the distance. As she dropped lower, she felt the engine give the slightest hiccup. She squinted at the fuel gauge. It sat in the red.

Another light! Was it a ship in the channel, or land?

More lights came up as the small coastal town responded to descending night.

The engine hiccupped again as she frantically searched for any place flat enough for her to land.

It coughed again, and the engine bucked, then caught, only to hiccup twice more.

There! A field, flat and empty with the crop taken in. Grace throttled back, dumping altitude and speed as safely as she could. The plane continued to choke as she lined up.

She'd told Dix they might not make it. Or, if they made it, they might crash into the sea. They might die.

He'd flashed a smile. She loved that smile.

"We'll make it."

She prayed he was right. The ground approached with terrifying speed as Grace fought to keep the wings level. The engine coughed its last, and fell silent.

Now she fought the rudder as the ground rushed toward them.

The landing was the worst she'd ever made. A tree she hadn't seen snapped the wing, skewing them sideways. One of the tires blew as the plane shuddered, canting sideways.

It stopped and she shouted as relief flooded her like a tidal wave. "We did it!"

"Grace!" She heard Dix calling, and struggled to unfasten the harness with fingers gone numb from gripping the controls. "GRACE?!"

She rose, aching in every muscle, and climbed down, only to be swept up into Dix's arms the moment her feet touched the ground.

Throwing back her head, she laughed. "Put me down, you crazy fool!" she said, loving the feel of his arms around her. Feet on English soil, safe, she held onto him for all she was worth.

"You did it!" he enthused, covering her face with kisses. In the distance, church bells rang.

"Dix, the bells."

"A church. We can get help there."

"It's Christmas Eve."

He looked down into her eyes and smiled.

"Will you marry me there, Grace? In whatever little church, in whatever little town this is?"

"Yes, oh yes," she said, kissing him once more. "Right here, where we came home."

"I love you Lady Grace Corvedale."

"I love you, Lt. Robert Dixon."

Together they turned toward the sound of the bells.

"Merry Christmas, my love," he said, as they started walking.

"Welcome Home."

ABOUT THE AUTHOR

Jeanne Adams likes calling North Carolina home, but for now, she lives in DC, where her latest full-length novel, THE TENTACLE AFFAIRE (Sept. 2014), is set. She often jogs on the C&O towpath with her dogs, just like the heroine in that particular book! Her favorite holiday is Halloween and she starts planning the annual yard decor spectacle on November 1. Alas, in this case however, "The Adams Family" - one husband, two sons and three dogs - is all bark and no bite.

On another spooky and suspenseful note, Jeanne used to work in the funeral and cemetery business, and knows a thing or two about getting rid of the body....bwhahahah! (She even teaches classes about it for writers!) She claims that's one reason she took up writing romantic suspense!

Jeanne has written award-winning suspense novels for Kensington/Zebra Publishing since 2007, including the highly acclaimed DEADLY LITTLE SECRETS, and its follow up, DEADLY LITTLE LIES.

THE TENTACLE AFFAIRE is her first urban fantasy/romance. The recently published DEADLY DELIVERY (Nov. 2014) is a short romantic suspense novella set at Thanksgiving, and BEHIND ENEMY LINES, the novella first published in A JEWEL IN TIME, is her first novella in an anthology.

She loves hearing from readers, so find her in any of the following places:

On her website - www.JeanneAdams.com where you can sign up for her newsletter.

Follow her on Twitter @JeanneAdams

48680730R00102

Made in the USA
Middletown, DE
25 September 2017